White Wolf Woman

White Wolf Woman

Native American Transformation Myths
Collected and Retold by

Teresa Pijoan

August House Publishers, Inc.
LITTLE ROCK

Published by August House, Inc.,
P.O. Box 3223, Little Rock, Arkansas 72203,
501-372-5450.

Printed in the United States of America

10 9 8 7 6 5 4 3 2 1

LIBRARY OF CONGRESS CATALOGING-IN-PUBLICATION
DATA

White wolf woman : Native American transformation myths /
collected and retold by Teresa Pijoan. p.   cm.
Summary : A collection of thirty-seven transformation myths collected
from the oral traditions of Native Americans, showing the powers of
certain animals as they move between human and nonhuman worlds.
ISBN 0-87483-201-2 (alk. paper) : $17.95
ISBN 0-87483-200-4 (pbk.: alk. paper) : $8.95
1. Indians of North America—Legends. 2. Metamorphosis—Folklore.
3. Human-animal relationships—North America—Folklore.
[1. Indians of North America—Legends. 2. Animals—Folklore.] I.Title.
E98.F6P54   1992
[398.2]—dc20   92-5269

First Edition, 1992

Executive: Liz Parkhurst
Design director: Ted Parkhurst
Cover design: Byron Taylor
Typography: Lettergraphics / Little Rock

This book is printed on archival-quality paper which meets the
guidelines for performance and durability of the Committee on
Production Guidelines for Book Longevity of the
Council on Library Resources.

AUGUST HOUSE, INC.   PUBLISHERS   LITTLE ROCK

To George and Thelma Breen,
with appreciation to
John Laughing Eyes DeLong,
who holds the Raven's song.

Contents

Introduction

A cold winter wind blows around a centuries-old adobe house north of Albuquerque, once a waystation on the Santa Fe road. Inside, we sit around a warm fire with Teresa Pijoan, discussing her book of transformation myths. The collection of stories is unique, and so is the teller.

Teresa Pijoan was born in Española, New Mexico, the daughter of Dr. Michel and Barbara Pijoan, and the granddaughter of essayist José Pijoan, the most famous writer in Spain of the 1930s. Her family ran the general store at San Juan Pueblo in the three decades ending when the store burned in 1973, and her father was the doctor for the pueblo. In the store the elder women who came to shop stayed to visit and began to recognize Teresa's gifts as a storyteller.

Teresa fit in well with the good people of San Juan Pueblo, and learned their language and folkways. She participated in the dances and in the puberty rites for young women. She learned the Tewa language—and other languages as well, later—and learned the stories of the San Juan people the way her Indian companions did, often working one-on-one with an elder of the pueblo. When the pueblo chose eight young people to become trusted storyholders, there were seven boys and one young woman in the pithouse, or *kiva,* for the ceremonials: Teresa received her new lifelong honor and obligation as a storyholder.

"When you become a storyholder," Teresa said, "you have a duty and obligation to retell the stories." *White Wolf Woman* is one result of a lifetime of learning, holding, telling, and sharing stories. Teresa holds more than six hundred stories from many different tribes, spanning like the rainbow bridge the landscape of Indian cultures. This anthology spans for its readers the gulf, like deep arroyos of the Southwest, separating European-American traditions from native American traditions.

All the world's cultures have used storytelling—sometimes in the form of myths, folktales, programmatic dances, or narrative songs—to explain human origins, interpret the natural world, preserve communal folkways and philosophies, and guide new generations along the pathway to productive inclusion in the adult world. Since the beginnings of human speech, it is the power of words that separates the young adult from the newborn, the human society from the society of animals, and one cultural group from another who do not speak the same language. All human societies acknowledge the power of words: for the Greeks that power was in Logos, the word and the wisdom that were the basis for reason and reality; for the Hebrews that power was manifest in the True Name of God, never spoken aloud; for some African societies the power resided in an individual's name, which was kept secret from the world at large, and a nickname used in its place; for the native American and many other cultures of the earth, that power is felt in what Margot Astrov calls "the magic creativeness of the word."

"The singing of songs and the telling of tales, with the American Indian," Astrov says, "is but seldom a means of mere spontaneous self-expression. More often than not, the singer aims with the chanted word to exert a strong influence and to bring about a change, either in himself or in nature or in his fellow beings."[1]

Rodney Frey expresses it thus: "Spoken words are not just semantic means of communication or descriptions of phenomena. They are also endowed with power that can affect the context in which they are expressed. In fact, words can bring about phenomena...." Frey concludes that the words and symbols of stories and songs are themselves "inundated with creative power."[2]

The native American transformation myths do not merely tell of transformations; they can bring about new transformations. They do not speak only of powers and testing of archetypal characters in the ancient times; they speak to the new generation of listeners and empower it with the means to bring about transformation in itself.

Teresa was first inspired to assemble this collection when, as a teacher at Canyon de Chelly, she enjoyed hearing the stories of her students from the Payute, Apache, Navaho, Pueblo, and other tribes. With the passing of years and the collecting of more stories, her attention was drawn to the striking similarities among the stories of her Pueblo friends, the other tribes, and even the European and Judeo-Christian traditions. The storytelling that was her community service at age eighteen—all Pueblo young people are expected to serve the community—has become Teresa's profession as well as her obligation. The stories from the Canyon de Chelly institutes, added to many she has learned at powwows, ceremonies, communions, weddings, summer camps, and at the San Juan Mercantile, form a cultural treasure of tremendous value. Although she has told them in schools, colleges, churches, kivas, state fairs, and the American Museum of Natural History, she realizes that publishing these stories will preserve them for the cultures from which they come, and introduce them to a wider audience, of more diverse cultural background, than she could reach through verbal telling alone.

"Another reason that I wrote this collection," Teresa told us, "is the fact that my daughters were growing up and changing as I was learning some of these stories, and I was so amazed at the transformations in their lives. I realized how, at the same time, as a parent I was also changing, and how we all change in our lives without being aware of it, and without being in control of that change. That was very profound to me." We all sat in silence, until Teresa spoke again. "In the Indian tradition we are on the path, and endeavoring to stay on the path, when testing comes to us, and we believe that we are on the right path, and that transformation is inevitable."

The inevitability of transformation is a key element in these stories. The European-American tradition often fears change, hence the appeal of Peter Pan. The native American stories accept change. The European-American listener expects the ending "they lived happily ever after"; the native American listener accepts "she lived for four days with her people before she became deathly ill and died." European-American stories often polarize good and evil; native American stories often show the dual nature of human beings and spirits, with a good side and an evil side.

Many storytelling conventions in Indian stories differ from the traditions of the non-Indian:

- While European stories repeat events in threes, Indian stories repeat events in fours.
- While European heroes are praised for succeeding, Indian heroes are honored for their attempt, even if they fail.
- When animals talk in European stories, they usually illuminate human foibles. When animals talk in Indian stories, it is because they are respected as equals in the natural world, with wisdom to share with human beings.

For the animals are, as Pacific Northwest Indian storyteller Johnny Moses puts it, "just people in animal clothing."

The common spirit shared by human beings and animals in the native American cosmos makes them equal partners in the natural world, and hunters must show respect for the spirits of their prey. The spirit world and "this world" are close, and all Indian people respect the ceremonies that link the two. The native American perception of the spirit world differs enough from that of the European-American that some comments might guide the reader to a fuller understanding:

- The spirit world and the natural world are so close that certain beings can move back and forth between the two almost effortlessly.
- The right side of the human body is linked with the natural world and the left side with the spirit world.
- The first people emerged from the mother earth through an opening into the natural world called by the Pueblo people the *Shi-pa-pu;* other tribes have similar "births" for mankind.
- The *Shi-pa-pu* also is the opening in the floor of the Pueblo ceremonial kiva through which spirits come into this world to guide, instruct, or punish disrespect.
- Just as spirits and other powerful beings can pass back and forth from the natural to the spirit world, so many beings in the natural world can pass back and forth from their human to animal forms.
- Passing into the spirit world, which non-Indians might regard as simply death, may represent the death of one level of consciousness and the rebirth of another.

Beyond these general comments, it is difficult to give the reader broad statements about the meaning of the stories or the qualities of the animals. Each tribe has its own distinct attitude toward certain animals. To one group a bear is wisdom, to another boorishness. To one tribe coyote is the creator-spirit, to another he is a cowardly prankster. Some folklorists and anthropologists issue broad, sweeping statements about pan-tribal beliefs, but Teresa never does so. As a storyholder, she must go to each tribal group respectfully to learn each different word, concept, clan name, and cultural nuance. Of course, some pan-tribal storytelling conventions exist:

- Many characters do not have names, stressing the universality of human experience.
- Most Indian languages lack a word for "myth," using simply "story."
- Most Indian storytelling is done with gesture and voice to enhance spoken sentences that are often verbally lean and very short when written.
- Many Indian stories presuppose some knowledge of tribal ways since they were originated to be told only to one specific tribe, and this may leave some aspects of some stories unexplained to the non-Indian reader.

As the fire was dying low, we asked what transformation this anthology might cause in the reader.

"A greater humility," Teresa answered. "Greater knowledge, awareness. A greater sensitivity to others and to other cultures. I've heard that 'education is what you remember after you've forgotten everything else.' What you remember from these stories is the power within that story, whatever it might be. In an oral society, every story connects each member of the society to every other. Life and the stories go on, and do not end."

As the moon came up, we talked of how Teresa first heard the story of White Wolf Woman when she was four years old, and our friend John told of the most recent sighting of White Wolf Woman, along the mesa, near Acoma Pueblo. Outside, it began to snow.

—*Richard and Judy Dockrey Young*
HARRISON, ARKANSAS

Notes

1. Margot Astrov, *American Indian Prose and Poetry* (New York: Capricorn Books, 1962), 19.

2. Rodney Frey, *The World of the Crow Indians: As Driftwood Lodges* (Norman: University of Oklahoma Press, 1987), 163.

A Note from Teresa Pijoan

The transformation of life continues daily. Many are transformed, though few of us sense the spiritual means of the changes. These are the Old Ones' stories, holding the magic of the land. The power of the story is in the feeling it portrays—and the passage of that feeling brings transformation.

The Navaho tell of the order of Animal Heroes. First Man planned to build a home. He dug a shallow pit in Earth Mother; the raised dirt was pushed against the main poles. One of the main poles First Man used was the Black Bow, called *Altqin-dilqil,* or First Hogan Pole. The parts of this Black Bow were cut from the Male Reed Strip and one from the Female Reed Strip. They were known as the Slayers of Those who Attack us Bringing Evil.

The whole structure was covered up with earth. Grass was planted on the roof. This was the First Dwelling. First Woman ground white corn into meal, and she and First Man sprinkled it inside the First Hogan. They sprinkled it from East to West.

First Man spoke as he spread the cornmeal. "May this First Hogan be sacred, may it be filled with beauty, and may the days be plenty."

This is the First Hogan ceremony. After the First Hogan was built, they had four dark and four light clouds. First Man said that they should rest. He asked if anyone had gathered river stones. Badger said that he had five river stones. First Man heated them. He built two sacred houses out of the remaining poles. They chanted four chants in the house where the stones were heated to get the evil out. Then everyone sang a song:

> *He made it a place where the people rose up from the*
> *   underworld;*
> *Near the Lake of Emergence, He made it;*
> *He made it with the wood from the female and the wood*
> *   from the male;*
> *He made it with the Black Mesa rock;*
> *He made it with the hard, round river rock;*
> *He made it with the help of the All Creator.*

Everyone sang this song, even the Horned Toad, the Twin Brothers, the Bear, and the Turquoise Boy who is Neither Female nor Male. Transformation had begun, and with this the magic was set free upon the land along with the animals.

These stories were collected from all over the Americas and from different tribes and groups of native Americans. They are recorded to awaken us.

May you walk with the awareness of life.

May you walk in beauty.

—Teresa Pijoan
ALGODONES, NEW MEXICO

Snakes

Every animal is a spiritual powerholder in native American mythology. Snakes are supernatural beings and are believed to have special abilities. They can bring rain when there is drought, can bring flash floods of death and destruction, can emit power on another, and can remove the spirit from the dead and take it to the Other Place. Snakes are lightning, directions of arroyos, visionholders, spiritkeepers, and leaders of The People.

The horned snake is drawn on altars, pottery, wood, drums, and medicine bowls, and is woven into fabric. The Pueblo People do not kill snakes. In fact, if a person is bitten by a snake, the bite is blamed on something or someone else. The Snake medicine man takes the patient back to the ceremonial house of the Snake Society, where he is brought back to health over four days.

A patient who has gone through the Snake Society healing has the opportunity to join the group. Traditionally, the initiation ceremony lasted four or five days. First, the patient would give a packet of specially prepared prayer meal to the head of the Snake Society, who distributed it among the members. After the initiation ceremony, the Snake Society and family members moved to a little adobe house where the medicine men and women would sing and dance before the altar. The Head Healing Person of the Snake Society then went out, danced before the altar, and beckoned to the patient to come forward. He would be carried to the altar by his father, who held him up with eagle wing feathers. Then the singing would begin, and a medicine man from another society would come out and give the father and the patient each a live snake of a type related to the healing being effected. This demonstrated publicly that the patient had the option to become a member of the Snake Society.

Live snake ceremonies once were widespread among the Pueblo Indians. They were documented in 1581 and 1582 by Father Rodriquez and Captain Chamuscado at a then-functioning pueblo near Galisteo, New Mexico. The men wrote of two live rattlesnakes being carried by the dancers, who gave the snakes to a patient. The snakes coiled around the neck and body of that person. Antonio de Espejo also reported witnessing the ceremony at Acoma in 1583. Live snakes were kept in the pueblos for ceremonial purposes until just recently.

The Snake Society traditionally performed at the pueblos in both the wet summer ceremony and the dry winter ceremony. The Snake Society had two kinds of masks—No'wira, the snake, and **Mokaitc**, the mountain lion. Both men and women belonged to the Snake Society, performing the sacred healings and dancing in the snake-holding ceremony.

The Dakota Indians will not kill snakes by hitting them, and they believe that anyone who does will have horrible dreams about snakes and will be overtaken and harmed by the spirit of the snake. One Dakota Sioux grandfather at an outdoor powwow ceremony in Gallup, New Mexico, once said, "There are some spirits in a snake, and it is most unlucky *to dream of snakes. They are terrible; they seek to enter a man's ears, nose, or mouth; and if a snake should succeed at this, it is death. No good comes from thinking of snakes."*

The Guiana Indians of South America, like the North American Indians, believe that spirits take on anthropomorphic forms. The Snake Spirits are good or bad and can help or harm. People can be relieved of an evil-presence power through the use of a rattle or by blowing through a male reed pipe.

There is the belief that an animal which regularly changes its skin will live forever. A grandmother from Guiana who was visiting a family in San Juan Pueblo, New Mexico, sang a song that went: "You will always be young like snakes if you change your skins, or you shall die. Kururumanni [Creator] came down to earth to see what the Arawaks were doing. They were bad, very bad, and he destroyed them by taking away their everlasting life. They could no longer change their skins. This great virtue he blessed upon the snakes, lizards, and cockroaches."

Snakes hold the power of the underworld, this world, and the spirit world. They demand respect and are not specifically good or bad, holy or evil, but uniquely named, uniquely individualistic among different groups of people, and deeply respected. Here, then, are some of their stories.

1. Thunder Son

The eastern woodlands of the United States hold a story of an Algonquin woman who lived alone at the edge of a village. This young woman washed and combed her long, brown-black hair with oils from animals, and her body was plump with their meat. She carried heavy chopped wood to her home alone, nurturing her strength every day. Her skin was smooth as corn silk, for she washed in the cold river water only once in a great while. Her clothes were washed in the river and left to dry lying on the bushes in the hot sun.

She was beautiful. She knew she was beautiful. She was too beautiful to have just any man. She stayed by herself with her own admiration. She worked alone in the cornfields and returned, noticing her reflection in the water baskets that she carried. She lived alone in her beauty. Then one day she met a man.

This man was like no one she had ever known. His strength shone in his deep, piercing, brown-black eyes. This man had followed her from the river path back to her home. His long, black hair blew behind him as he walked beside her. He took the water baskets from her hands. His sleek, muscular body rippled as he walked beside her. His power echoed with his long stride.

The feathers tied in his hair lifted with each step. His voice echoed through the air as he spoke. "Maiden, let me help you with your water-carrying. Let me invite you to my home to meet my family."

She followed him. She would not look into his eyes, yet she smiled. He walked beside her to his mother's wigwam. He introduced her to his two sisters, and they asked her to remain. She stayed with these people, for they appreciated her and needed her company. She accepted this strong man as her man and became one of them.

Her man would go out hunting all day while the women worked in the fields. He brought home plenty of meat, for he was an excellent hunter. The women were magical in their growing of corn, so there was always much corn bread, corn stew, and cornmeal. Life was good in this way.

One day, the man came back later than usual—his hands bloody with cuts, his hair tangled in snarls, his moccasins torn. He told his story: "The hunt this day was difficult—the deer was quick. I shot and only wounded it. I prayed and followed it, but the deer ran to the sacred stream and ate plants that heal. Then it rolled in the sacred mud and the wound disappeared.

I knew that I was not to kill this one. I returned to the hunting field and prayed to find another deer.

"The deer that came across the field was an older stag. It stared at me, and I knew that this stag would be the one killed. It was a fine deer with horns of great honor and a sleekness of spirit. Then the stag leapt over the hedge and was gone. I was fast, and agile, and soon found the tracks leading over the edge of a high cliff. But I did not notice the cliff, only the tracks.

"My body was badly bruised, hands cut, legs ripped as I freed myself from the hedge of thorns that saved me. I limped home without meat."

He was tired. He lay down on his bedroll with his head on his beautiful woman's lap. She stroked his hair, feeling the weariness of his spirit. She noticed that his body was transforming. His breathing slowed as he turned into a gigantic snake. The beautiful woman felt the hair she was stroking shrink to scales that covered his head. She carefully inched her way out from under his massive, fanged head to escape outside.

His mother saw this woman's fearful expression. "We are Serpent-People. We are good and wish you well. My son truly loves you; yet if you feel that you can no longer stay here, then you should run away. But go quickly, for if my son wakes and knows that you have run from him, he will try to find you and bring you back. Run, run, and go quickly. Do not look back."

The beautiful woman ran. Her legs moved quickly at first; then as she thought of her good man, his kindnesses, his abilities, she slowed. Her mind argued with her heart. She sat down to rest. She was tired and decided to close her eyes and pray. She had a dream. She dreamt that her pride was what brought her into this problem and that her wisdom would get her home. She awoke in a thunderstorm.

Thunder Spirit called to her, and the deep, rolling voice was deafening. She jumped up with her hands over her ears. The great voice echoed across the land: "RUN, RUN, RUN! THE SNAKE-MAN IS BEHIND YOU! HE SHALL

CATCH YOU!" The beautiful woman ran with the fear of her soul pounding in her head. She heard the terrible rustling of the serpent-man.

She let her legs move her across the mountains, and soon she came to a lake near her home. There, standing around the lake, were three handsome men. The tallest put out his hand, telling her to stop. He lifted his long, shining spear at the serpent, threw it, and pierced the snake. All at once a roaring black cloud surrounded the three men. The tallest spear thrower was a Thunderman.

The Thundermen took the woman to their father's home on an island. She married the third son, who was kind, quiet, and thoughtful. She gave birth to a baby boy. The boy grew strong and used his thunder well. The woman asked Thunder Father if she could go home for a visit and take her son with her to meet her people. Thunder told her that she could take her son with her as long as he never used arrows. His son's arrows would turn to lightning and destroy people. The woman agreed.

At first their life went well. Thunderboy was quiet and stayed close to his mother. The other children stayed away from him for they did not know him. Then they began to jeer at him and laugh at him, saying that he did not know how to use an arrow or a bow. This made Thunderboy angry. He took a bow and an arrow and shot wide. It hit some trees and started a terrible fire. His grandfather swooped down and carried the boy to the sky where he is unable to hurt men.

The woman stayed with her people. She lives alone and works with the other women. Her beauty is no longer of interest to her, and she warns others to look into the heart for beauty.

2. Spirit Eggs

There were two young Cheyenne men known for their eagerness to travel and to learn of new ideas. Everyone respected them, for they had a great talent for exploring and returning with wonderful stories. These two were unique. The older one was very quiet. He noticed the change in the leaves as the trees grew each year. It was said that he could tell if there was to be a rainstorm by talking with grasses in the dry gullies. He was called Quiet Listener.

The younger traveler talked most of the time. He shared his knowledge with anyone, and if there was no one to share it with, he spoke out loud to himself. His name was Spirit Seeker.

Quiet Listener did not mind his friend's constant talk. It allowed him to concentrate further. For he always knew where his friend was by the sound of his voice. These two close friends traveled far, but they always returned before the winds came. That is, until they came to the place of Spirit Food.

The day had started out as any other day. The two friends had slept out in the open, then had hunted for breakfast and found nothing. They continued to travel, searching for food and new wonders. Their hunger increased by late in the day and they became intent on finding food. Spirit Seeker came to a small stream. He crouched in the grass, hoping to spear a fish or perhaps a frog. There was no sign of movement anywhere on that stream. The young man crawled around in the grass, disappointed that there wasn't a single food source. Then, as he bent over the water, he touched something in the tall grass with his cupped hand.

There in the tall grass was a nest, and it was most peculiar. He called to Quiet Listener, who came and studied the eggs. They were quite large—larger than any bird's egg he had ever seen. He studied the markings on the eggs. It was most unusual.

"Can we eat them? They are all right to eat, aren't they?" asked Spirit Seeker.

Quiet Listener studied Spirit Seeker's face. "You are very hungry, and they are here. If you want to eat one and find out, go ahead. I don't know what they are, or who they belong to."

Spirit Seeker cracked the bottom of the egg and let the nourishment fall into his mouth. "It is delicious. Here, try one!" he said, handing an egg to his friend.

"No, I do not feel the hunger as you do," answered Quiet Listener. "You go ahead and eat them."

So Spirit Seeker ate all the eggs.

Quiet Listener started a small fire and they slept that night near the stream. In the morning, they heard the call of the winds. It was time to return home. They covered the fire and started on their way. The wind blew against them. Spirit Seeker started to limp.

"My legs hurt in this wind. Could we sit down and rest?" Quiet Listener found a place that was out of the wind. They sat for some time while Spirit Seeker rubbed his legs.

By midday, they were on their way again. Quiet Listener found berries and wild squash, which they ate. They continued to walk. Spirit Seeker fell behind. He sat down on a rock and rubbed his legs. He shook his head.

"The pain in my legs is very bad. I think I should put them in water if we find a stream. I will swim and let the water remove the pain."

They headed to a small river. There Spirit Seeker took off his loincloth and jumped into the water. He swam, while Quiet Listener hunted for firewood and food. Spirit Seeker swam and swam. The sun moved across the sky and soon was setting on the horizon.

"Get out of the water! The cold air will be coming and your legs will feel worse. Get out of the water!" Quiet Listener called from shore.

Spirit Seeker pulled his arms and upper body onto the land. He moved his legs to lift them out of the water, but he no longer had legs. They were one long tail. It was colorful, with red and black striped rings.

Spirit Seeker called out to his friend, "What has happened to my legs? What has happened to me?" Quiet Listener said nothing. That night they ate their food quietly.

In the morning, Quiet Listener took leaves and grasses, wove them into a thick, wet blanket, and wrapped Spirit Seeker's tail with it. He lifted up his friend and carried him on his back.

After several hours, Spirit Seeker said, "I cannot travel this way. I need to be in water."

Quiet Listener could hear the rasping sound of his friend's breathing. The wet leaf blanket was moving slowly on his back—not as if the body were moving, but as if it were changing shape. Quiet Listener thought of the magic that he was bearing. He continued to carry Spirit Seeker, who was silent and slept.

As the day grew warmer, Quiet Listener found a stream. He put his sleeping friend down, unrolled the blanket, and rolled him into the water. He sat and watched as Spirit Seeker dove and swam.

Spirit Seeker swam to Quiet Listener and with a deep and rolling voice spoke. "I had a dream in the water. I am not to be here, but am to go to the large river. I am being called by the water spirits. Can you help me get there?"

Quiet Listener studied the face of his lifetime friend. Spirit Seeker's eyes were glazed over. There were no eyelids. His face was rounded, and the skin had become leathery. "I will help you," he answered. "I will carry you."

Quiet Listener carefully wrapped Spirit Seeker in the wet blanket of grasses and leaves. He lifted him once more onto his back. Spirit Seeker was heavier now. He was rounder and harder to hold. Quiet Listener carried him all day to the southeast, walking slowly and carefully. He missed his young friend's constant chatter. He missed Spirit Seeker.

The winds no longer blew. The sky was clear, watching, guiding the two friends. The sun stayed in the sky longer, giving them time to travel. The cold evening winds blew across Quiet Listener's face to let him know that they had arrived at the large river, the Mississippi River. Quiet Listener let Spirit Seeker roll off his back into the high grass, and he watched as his friend wriggled awkwardly. Spirit Seeker slithered out of the wet leaf blanket and crawled to the water's edge.

Spirit Seeker turned and spoke. "Do not be afraid, for we are friends. The spirits have made me. They have called me here to be the Holder of the River. If the people are in need, or travel by this stream, ask them to drop gifts into the water and I will help them. You are a true friend; you will always be in my prayers and with my spirit."

Spirit Seeker became Snake-Man, guardian of the Mississippi River. And when the Cheyenne came, they dropped tobacco, food, and other gifts to him. It is said he still is there.

3. Snake-Boy

There was a Cherokee boy who used to go bird hunting every day. He brought home his catch to give to his grandmother. She was very fond of him and appreciated his skill. This made the others in the family angry. They did not like the grandmother giving all her affection to this one boy, and they teased and tormented him for being the favorite. One day, he decided that he would find a way to leave them.

He told his grandmother not to be sad. The next morning, he did not eat anything and went off hungry and alone to the woods, where he stayed all day. In the evening, he returned, bringing with him a pair of deer horns. He went to the summer house and told his grandmother that he must be alone all that night. She went into a different house where the others were sleeping.

Early the next day, she went to the summer house to be with her favorite grandson. All she saw was a tremendous *uktena* (snake) with horns on its head, two human legs, and an immense body. He spoke to her and told her to leave him alone. She moved to the door but stayed close.

When the sun moved high in the sky, the immense snake moved out of the summer house. It grew and grew, making a horrible hissing sound and frightening all the people. It crawled through the village, then disappeared into the river.

The grandmother cried out in pain. She loved her grandson and he was gone. Her family told her that if she thought so much of this boy, she should go and stay with him. So she walked into the river and disappeared.

A man fishing nearby saw the grandmother sitting on a large rock in the river. She looked as she had always looked, but as soon as she saw him, she jumped into the water and was gone.

This fisherman decided to wait and see if the grandmother would rise out of the water again. When nighttime came, he fell asleep beside the river and had a dream of two hunters. They could not find any animal that was worth killing for meat, so one hunter decided that he would kill a squirrel. The other warned him of the taboo: if one ate squirrel meat, he would turn into a snake. But the first hunter just laughed.

He killed the squirrels, skinned them, roasted them, and ate until he was full. In the middle of the night, the other hunter heard a horrible groaning. He sat up and watched as his squirrel-eating friend cried out in pain. His companion now had the body and tail of a large water snake, and he was calling for help. But the other could not help him. He could only watch as the squirrel-eating hunter's body grew round and his head became a serpent's head. Soon the great snake crawled away to sink into the bed of the river.

The fisherman remembered this dream, and he went back to the village and told the people. They believed him.

4. Water Monster Snake-Man

The Chiricahua Apache once camped near Deming, New Mexico. There was a certain water hole nearby, where it was believed that spirits would come out and grab the people gathering water. They would never be seen again.

There was once a girl, sixteen years of age, who lived near this water hole with her family. There had been a terrible drought, and she—who was strong minded—feared that if she did not get water, her family would die of thirst. She visited the water hole with her pitch jar, using grass as a stopper and returning secretly to her family. She prayed to the spirit that dwelt in the water.

Her family carefully rationed the water and did well for a while. Then the mother became very ill, and again they were in desperate need of water. The daughter took the jar, hid it under her dress, and sneaked out at first dawn to get more water. She did not tell anyone where the water was from, nor did she want them to know. She cautiously hid her tracks as she hurried to the water hole. She filled her water jar, gathered grass to stuff in as a stopper, and started to leave—falling, instead, to her knees in prayer. A shadow fell over her and she disappeared.

The family awoke and wondered where their daughter had gone. They waited until midday and then began to search. The mother was now very ill and did not regain her strength. That evening, the young girl's mother went to the other world.

The family was now desperate to find the daughter. They searched everywhere, and finally a brother found her tracks leading to the water hole. The grandmother told the others to return home, that she would stay there and pray. Then she knelt at the water hole and sang her songs all night.

As the sun rose over her in the morning, a vision appeared to the old woman. The vision spoke to her: "Your granddaughter is safe. She is in good health. Go back to her people and tell them to pray and sing."

The grandmother hurried back with her message. The people held a ceremony. They sang, prayed, and chanted for the girl. One of the medicine men spoke to the father. "You are the father of the girl. You should go to the water hole and stay there. As the sun rises high, you shall see your daughter."

The father loved his daughter. He took some food and walked to the water hole. He gave the food as a gift, sang praises of the water hole, and sang of his love for his daughter. As the sun moved high in the sky, the day became very hot. The father continued to sing.

A man walked out of the water and came to him. He had long, black hair and one eye that was as bright as the moon. He stood in front of the father, who rose and greeted him. The man stood aside, and there behind him was the daughter. She was radiant. Her hair blew in the breeze. Her eyes sparkled with love and wisdom. Her face glowed with peace. "Father, I am living with this one. I live in a place where there is great beauty. I shall help you if you are in need; shall protect you if you are in danger; shall always be here for you. I must return to my place with my man."

She turned and walked back to the water hole, and the man waited for her to descend. As he entered the water, his body turned into a giant water snake. He disappeared under the water without so much as a ripple.

The father stayed there with his family. They killed many deer when they were hungry. They found caves to hide in when the Mexicans attacked. They had water when the earth was dry. Even so, the father watched his other children leave—and he finally decided to go as well. He went to the south and was killed by raiding Mexicans. It is said that his daughter still waits for his return to the water hole.

5. Rattlesnake Father

The Pomo people tell of a place known as Cobowin—a large rock with a hole in the center. At one time, many rattlesnakes lived inside this rock, and a Pomo village called Kalesima was near it.

Many families lived in Kalesima. There were four large houses and one that was right in the middle. The center house had an upright pole down through the roof to the floor—no one knew why.

A young maiden lived with her family in the pole house. She was hardworking, and her mother and father were proud of her. She was courted by many men, but her interests were her work, her family, and the ceremonies.

One day, this young maiden went searching for berries to use in a dye for a belt she wanted to weave. She studied each plant, unaware of her closeness to the Rock of Snakes. A large male snake was sunning himself on this rock, and he noticed the maiden. She was strong, her face was intense, and she held a beauty that he wanted. The rattlesnake disappeared down a hole in the rock.

The maiden bent down to gather berries. Her back hurt. She carried her heavy basket of berries on her hip as she tried to straighten her stiff back.

"Can I help you carry those berries?" a tall man asked, walking up to her. She turned to meet him and said, "I can carry them." Then she lowered her gaze, for to look into a man's eyes was a sign of bonding.

"I live to the south of here with my family," he said. "Your back appears to be hurt. I can carry the berries while you rest it."

The young maiden handed him the basket of berries, for he had a gentle quality. They walked side-by-side until they came to the village of Kalesima. The man followed her to the house, but she stopped him at the door. "You must not come in. You have not been invited." The young man stopped and looked down, as was polite.

"My parents will say if you can stay for dinner." She went into the main room while the young man waited with the basket of berries. He noticed the nice weavings on the wall. The warmth of the house felt good, for the fall wind was chilly.

The maiden returned and took the basket of berries. "Please come in," she said, "and meet my mother and father." Then she led him into a room filled with pots, baskets, and shields. The young man sat on a blanket next to her father, and he received a flat bowl of food. He thanked the parents for the invitation, and they made him feel quite comfortable.

The cold fall winds began to blow hard as the night progressed. The father insisted that the young man stay the night, and he accepted. But early next morning when the family awoke, the young man was gone.

Each day for four days, the young man came to the maiden's home. He brought her berries of many colors. He came with meat, feathers, and wonderful stories to share.

The maiden became curious about this young man. She would ask him of his parents and he would laugh and speak about hers. She would ask him about his home, but he would only shake his head and compliment her.

The morning of the fifth day was dark and cloudy, and it was a busy time for the young maiden's family. They were preparing for a feast, with everyone going in and out. The mother was kneeling on the floor mixing food when she heard a voice behind her. She smiled for she knew it was the young man. She turned to greet him but could see no one.

In the dark, dim room, the mother took a stick from the fire and lifted it up to see. There, on the floor where the voice was coming from, lay a large, coiled snake. She dropped the stick and ran for help, and soon the father came with neighbors. The mother led them into the room, but there was only the burned stick.

They searched for the daughter, but no one from the village could find her that day.

The maiden's curiosity had taken her to the snake rock. She waited, wanting the man to answer her questions. But when he walked to her, his eyes were round and he looked somehow different. She asked him if she could see his home and meet his family. He turned his head and, as he turned, took hold of her, coiling into a snake and squeezing her body. She went limp.

When she awoke, she was under the large rock in a dark underground room. All around her were snakes. "You wanted to see where I live and meet my family? Here they are."

The maiden peered around her. Snakes coiled, crawled, and caressed her. Heavy, thick snakes slithered down her legs. Thin, multi-colored snakes wiggled through her hair. Small, plain snakes crawled under her dress. Snakes were in her hands, around her toes, falling from her arms, and moving between her legs.

"Don't be afraid. They are curious. They need to know you, for you shall live here with us forever. You are now one of us." The young maiden looked into Snake-Man's eyes. He was the same person that she had been attracted to when they first met.

His tongue darted out and he said, "You have taken the oath of bonding by staring into my eyes. We are one."

The maiden had no choice, so she stayed with Snake-Man. They had many children, and sometimes Snake-Man let her go for walks above the rock with them.

The Snake children grew and asked many questions. They did not understand why their mother was different, but she explained that she was human. Her children were frightened of human beings, and there were times when they would strike people. Their mother taught them humility and understanding.

Snake-Man took great care to keep his woman away from her kind. Still, he noticed that as his woman aged, she grew sad. One evening, he asked her if she would like to visit her mother and father again. She eagerly said, "Yes."

Snake-Man took his woman out of the large rock and placed her on the pole above the roof of her parents' home. She climbed down into the main room. Her parents were overjoyed, and she stayed the evening with them. Then she had to leave, saying that she would never see them again and that she must return to her family.

The mother fell at her daughter's feet. "No, No, No, you are my beautiful daughter. Stay, or we will die without you. Please do not go, for my strength goes with you! Stay here!"

Snake-Man's woman shook as she tried to free herself from her mother's grip. And as she shook, her body faded, faded, faded until there was nothing at all. She was never seen again. Some say she turned into a snake and lives with her family under the large rock. Others say that in her grief she was taken away by the spirits.

6. Woman Seeker

White Corn was a young man who lived alone outside a Hopi Pueblo farming area. White Corn had six other brothers. They were named Red Corn, Blue Corn, Yellow Corn, Green Corn, Spotted Corn, and Black Corn. He decided that his life would be fuller if he had a woman. But a worthy woman would be hard to find, for White Corn held within him the knowledge of the spirit world, the strength of manhood, and the spirit of adventure.

White Corn gathered up his sacred cornmeal pouch with four feathered prayer sticks. White Corn walked until he reached a place of running water. *Daw-wa* the Sun Father met White Corn as the day ended and asked him to tie his four prayer sticks together, sending them afloat on the water. White Corn did as he was told by *Daw-wa* the Sun Father. White Corn sat thoughtfully and waited.

Soon a raft floated to him with four gigantic feathers for a sail. *Daw-wa* the Sun Father told White Corn that his woman was waiting for him on the land across the water, in the house of Great Snake Father. But *Daw-wa* the Sun Father warned White Corn that before he attempted the testing of Great Snake Father, he should befriend a rattlesnake who went by the name Big Rattle Man. Big Rattle Man would guide White Corn to Great Snake Father's home.

White Corn floated on his raft for fourteen days until he came to flat land. As White Corn got off, the raft shrank before him, and there on the water were his four prayer sticks. White Corn lifted them out of the water and walked across the land until he came to a mountain. There stood an old man.

This old man had no nose or mouth, and he was carrying a warped stick with a crook at the end. White Corn walked towards him, but suddenly the old man swung the hooked stick onto White Corn's arm. Before he could speak, he was being dragged up the mountain. Then White Corn fell forward, and when the old man stopped to look up, White Corn pulled away. At that moment, a terrible storm boomed out above them in the sky. The old man was hit with a long, yellow lightning snake and fell sprawled on the ground—but he was not hurt for he was a spirit.

White Corn ran. White Corn ran in the rain, lightning, and thunder until he fell. The old man caught him and grabbed his hand.

Then the old man placed a sharp obsidian knife in White Corn's hand and yelled into his face over the loud thunder, "Cut my forehead open! Cut my forehead open all the way down to my chin. Do not lift the blade once you start. Do not turn away. Once you have cut to the chin, take the blade and cut from ear to ear in one swift gesture. Do not turn away! Be strong!"

White Corn knelt in the rain and mud. He studied the strange face before him. The old man knelt with his eyes closed. White Corn felt the heat of the sharp obsidian knife.

He lifted the knife to the old man's forehead and cut deeply into the skin. There was no blood. White Corn pushed the blade to the chin.

The old man did not move nor speak. White Corn took the knife and placed it at the base of the old man's ear. He held the back of the head with his other hand and cut the skin. There was no blood. White Corn cut clean across to the other ear.

The old man's face peeled away. Skin peeled from the face and fell from the neck, and the old, withered body washed away in the rain. There in front of White Corn knelt a strong young man, saying, "You are no longer my captive. We are now friends. You have released me."

The thunderous clouds rolled out of the sky and the lightning disappeared. The two men laughed as they walked down the mountain, studying each other as they went. White Corn followed this young man who had strength in his step and knowledge in his face. They walked until they came to a fast-flowing river. White Corn touched his belt and found the four prayer sticks still in place. He turned to ask his companion if this river had a crossing, but the young man had disappeared.

White Corn took some cornmeal from his pouch, sprinkled it upon the river, and waited. From behind him came a hissing. He turned, and there weaving in and out of the tall grass was a gigantic snake. Its head was eye level to White Corn, and its mouth was larger than White Corn's head. The snake slithered around White Corn—sun glittering off its multi-colored skin.

The snake spat at White Corn, "Take your prayer sticks and put them in the river."

White Corn did as he was told. The four prayer sticks quickly turned into a raft. White Corn got onto it, then traveled for four days down the river. White Corn was filled with hunger, but his spirit was strong. White Corn watched the stars and traveled along the river, looking at the land and feeling the movement of the raft. Suddenly the raft fell. The water dropped away. All he heard was the air around him.

The sun came up and White Corn saw that his raft was floating on the colors of a rainbow. He was not falling, but rising up to the foot of the mountain where he had met the old man. The raft suddenly crashed against the rocks. White Corn stood bruised, weak, trembling, and without any sense of direction. He stood waiting for a sign. A snake's head came out from underneath a rock.

It was a large, brown rattlesnake, an ordinary snake. "Big Rattle Man?" called out White Corn. "Big Rattle Man? Big Rattle Man, I have come to find you."

The rattlesnake stopped. White Corn opened his pouch, took some white cornmeal, and sprinkled it on the snake. The rattlesnake grew in size, and then it led him through a cave in the mountain to a large cavern. White Corn sprinkled cornmeal on the earth in the cavern and placed his four prayer sticks before the rattlesnake. Rattlesnake breathed upon them.

The rattlesnake faced White Corn and said, "You are White Corn. I was told of you. White Corn, you are to participate in the ceremonies. White Corn, draw a circle with your cornmeal, and your ceremony will be revealed to you." Then the rattlesnake slithered away.

White Corn took his cornmeal and sprinkled it in a circle on the ground. He did this four times. He made three intersecting lines, and where the points met there came the different rains and winds. White Corn knelt studying this. When he stood and looked around him, he was inside the mountain, and there was no opening. The cavern was warm. All around him were men and women in a circle. In the center sat an old man whom the people called Snake Father as they passed by him. Snake Father nodded to dancing people, but he stared at White Corn.

"You, White Corn, come here!" he said. "White Corn, come and meet the Snake Father."

Then he announced, "White Corn is here"—

We have been waiting for the one who will open the gates;
We have been waiting for the one who will let the sun into
our world;
We have been waiting for the one who will let the stars into
our world;
We have been waiting for the one who will go through the
testing of the Snake Order;
We have prayed for the one who can find freedom in
himself—find freedom for those who live in the dark.

White Corn was taken down a tunnel to another chamber—this one with a waterfall. The men took White Corn's loincloth from him. The men bathed White Corn in the water. The men washed White Corn's hair. They took White Corn's face in their hands and each stared into White Corn's eyes.

White Corn saw the loneliness in each one's eyes. They took White Corn's arms and felt the strength of his youth. They poured water over White Corn's strong chest. They rubbed the water over White Corn's abdomen, feeling the hunger within him. They rubbed White Corn's loins, feeling the power of White Corn's fathers. They rubbed White Corn's thighs, feeling his past. They rubbed White Corn's feet, feeling his presence. They washed White Corn.

White Corn noticed the skin of the old ones who stood around him. As they washed White Corn clean, his body lost its softness. In place of skin, there was a shiny, hard, shell-like covering; and the longer the old ones bathed White Corn and gave him their strength, the tighter and tougher his skin became. White Corn felt the hardness of their fingers and White Corn pulled away from the old ones.

Then Snake Father entered the cavern and told White Corn that he was to choose a woman. White Corn was lifted out of the water. He walked in his nakedness to the room of women. White Corn looked into their eyes and saw nothing. White Corn could not choose one of these.

Then Snake Father reached up into the air, creating a bubble with a beautiful maiden inside. She became a young woman, walked naked from the bubble, and stood before White Corn.

Snake Father spoke to White Corn. "She is called Bright Eyes. She is for you." White Corn reached out his hand to her and she took it.

The people gathered. White Corn and his woman were clothed. The people danced. The people ate. The people sang songs. White Corn was given full initiate rites into the Snake Clan. And at last, the people grew weary. They lay on the floor of the cavern and slept. Snake Father led White Corn and Bright Eyes through a tunnel to the outside.

White Corn turned to speak to Snake Father. Snake Father was gone. So White Corn took Bright Eyes to the place of the *Fits-ki* (sun's rays), and the *Fits-ki* led them to his people. The people of the pueblo were in mourning, and they told White Corn of a terrible drought. Many had died. There was no food.

Bright Eyes went to the people the next day. Bright Eyes summoned the snakes, calling them to dance. Bright Eyes sang. The snakes rattled their rattles. The clouds rolled down from the mountains and covered the sky. Rain fell by day's end. The crops grew and all was well.

Bright Eyes was working outside when a storm came suddenly. Bright Eyes called to the people, telling them to go indoors. But Bright Eyes was caught by the rain. Bright Eyes called out to the rain, letting the moisture enter into her. Bright Eyes sang as the rain nurtured life within her, and soon Bright Eyes grew large with child.

White Corn knew of this, knew that it was very special magic. White Corn cared for his woman and took her up to the mountain. After seven days, White Corn and Bright Eyes returned with their children. White Corn and Bright Eyes had five snakes.

The people were frightened. They had a meeting and decided that they should kill the five snakes. They discussed how they would do this, for Bright Eyes and White Corn held the power of spirits. An old man appeared to the people, saying, "You must let me take the children. I will care for them and they will not harm you." The people gave him the five snakes.

The old man placed the snakes in his house. Late that night, a thick smoke came from there, and screams of horrific pain. The old man was never seen again.

In the morning, the five snakes returned to their mother. Bright Eyes took her five snakes to the valley, covering their trail and not looking back at the village. Bright Eyes and her five snakes were never seen again.

White Corn waited for Bright Eyes to return. White Corn taught the people of Bright Eyes' rain ceremony and taught them respect for the snakes and their power. White Corn put the men through testings until they learned the power of the snake dance and became the Snake Clan.

White Corn waited for his woman to return, but Bright Eyes did not come back to him. Finally, White Corn decided that it was time for him to take another woman. So White Corn found one of great strength and with her founded the White Corn Clan, which became the largest among his people. White Corn grew old. White Corn taught the people wisdom. White Corn cared for his strong wife.

At last, Sun took White Corn away from the people. Sun now has White Corn in the sky with the other spirits. Yet the people remember. The people of the Snake Clan are still here, and they remember.

7. Water Jar Boy

There were people living at Sikyatki, a pueblo in New Mexico. Among them was a young Tewa Pueblo maiden who refused to be married. She was very plain and had to be told when to do her chores. She was an only child and her mother's helper.

Her father hunted now and then. He gathered food now and then. He was an official in the village now and then. He was filled with laughter and warmth.

The maiden's mother worked all the time. She made water jars all the time. She was stern, strict, and filled with severity all the time. She never smiled.

This daughter helped her mother make the clay water jars. The maiden learned of the suffering that came from hard work. The maiden learned of the importance of her place. The maiden learned of her plainness, and learned to live without suitors. The maiden learned to live with her parents as the years went by.

One day, the mother was mixing clay and realized that she needed more water. She told her daughter to mix the clay while she went to the river. As the daughter stamped her feet in the mud, it splattered on her calves, her thighs, and entered her. The daughter was afraid of the mud; the daughter tried to pull it off, and tried to get it out of her. The daughter cried out as she pushed the mud deeper into her body.

When her mother returned with the water, the daughter was giving birth to a water jar. The mother stood in disbelief. The mother was angry. The mother scolded her daughter, yelled, and asked how this could have happened. Other women gave birth to babies, but her daughter gave birth to a water jar.

The daughter cried and cried and cried and cried. Her mother picked up the jar to fling it to the ground when the water jar cried, "Feed me, feed me. I am hungry!" The mother knelt and pumped her daughter's breasts, letting the milk fall into the mouth of the water jar, which gurgled as the milk entered it. The mother decided to take the jar and her daughter home.

The daughter cried and cried and cried and cried, and the mother told her to be quiet. The water jar cried out in its hunger. The mother pumped her daughter's breast, letting the milk fall into the jar, which drank and cried for more. The daughter cried and cried and cried and cried.

Her father came in and learned of his grandchild, the water jar. He laughed and was most pleased, for he had always wanted a grandchild. He held the water jar and sang to it. He became very fond of the water jar, but its mother only cried and cried and cried and cried.

The water jar grew, and in twenty days it had become very large. It played with the other children, who became very fond of it. When it learned to talk, the children found out that their friend was a water jar boy. The mother cried and cried and cried and cried, for her son had no legs, arms, eyes, or face. The grandmother clicked her tongue. She was still angry with her daughter.

The snows came. It was time for the grandfather to go rabbit hunting, and Water Jar Boy begged to go along, too. Grandfather loved Water Jar Boy and consented. His mother cried and cried and cried and cried.

So Grandfather took him hunting, and he rolled along as the old man walked. Soon he saw rabbit tracks and followed them. But when a rabbit ran out of the hole, Water Jar Boy was startled, and he rolled back quickly and hit a large rock. The water jar broke and out jumped a real boy, glad that he had broken his tight clay skin. He grew, and soon he was covered with white buckskin, layers of beaded necklaces, an earstring of turquoise, a dance kilt, moccasins, and a buckskin shirt.

He killed four jack rabbits and returned to his grandfather, who was frantic. "Where is my grandson, the water jar? Where could he have gone?"

"I am your grandson, and I have killed four rabbits."

"No, my grandson is a water jar."

The grandson told Grandfather what had happened, and they walked home to tell the two women. Water Jar Boy's mother met them at the door, thinking this young man had come to court her. She flirted with this suitor. Then Grandfather told them of the broken water jar, and the mother cried and cried and cried and cried.

The boy asked his mother who his father was, but she only cried and cried and cried and cried. So he went in search of his father, traveling east until he came to a spring. There he met a man and told him, "I am looking for my father."

"Would you know him if you saw him?" asked the man.

The boy answered, "*You* are my father."

The man nodded. "Yes, you are right," he said. "Come with me."

They traveled down into the spring, and there the boy's father introduced him to everyone and they had a good time. Then the boy remembered his mother and returned home, but his mother was very ill and she died. The boy felt there was no reason for him to stay in the empty house, so he went back to his father. There he found both his mother and father.

His father's name was Red Water Snake. He had entered the mud to find out about the people. When his woman had died, he brought her spirit to this place. They all live together, now.

8. Sacred Snake

The Zuni Indians of the Southwest speak of the majestic village under Thunder Loud Mountain. It was called the Place of the Eagles, but today there is only a skeleton ruin.

At one time, there was an elder in the Place of the Eagles. He was the Priest-Chief who held wisdom of the spirit world and sacred healing powers. He had many daughters, but one he could not understand. His oldest daughter was continually worried about being dirty, or about wearing soiled clothing. She washed her hands in water buckets kept by the door of her special, solitary, clean little house. She washed her body from dawn to dusk in the spring at the base of the village. She washed her hair whenever the wind blew. She had very little time for anything else but cleanliness.

The spring at the edge of the village was a sacred spring. People stayed away from it. Nearby was an altar place of offerings and prayer, so the sacred spring was not a place to bathe. The father had told his daughter this time and time again. She did not listen. The water in the spring was fresh, clear, and cool every day.

A drought came upon the land. Water became scarce, and this daughter no longer could get water from the fast-flowing river to wash her clothes. So she washed them in the sacred spring. When there was no water from the ground wells for cooking her food, she gathered water from the sacred spring. She bathed, washed, cooked, and drank the water from the sacred spring.

But the spring was not without life of its own. The dark hole that seeped Mother Earth's clear liquid held a creature, which was a coiled spirit keeping his watchful eye on the beauty who came to him. He watched her cautiously. He appreciated the curves of her body, her grace, and her love for the water. He waited.

The oldest daughter brought her tree-sap baskets to the sacred spring, submerging them deep into the water. The coiled spirit shrank away from the baskets, and then they disappeared. The spirit knew she would return.

He floated to the surface of the sacred spring, breathed in Father Sky's strength, and became a small human male infant. He knew that a human baby would drown in the water, and he cried out for help. The oldest daughter heard the crying. There, in the sacred spring, was a newborn infant. She lifted him out of the water and let him suckle her breast. Holding him, she searched for the mother, but there was no one. She took him to her clean little home and lay down with him. Soon the two of them were fast asleep.

The massive body of the powerful snake was cramped in the tiny infant's body. The snake breathed and grew, filling every space of the small, clean home. The oldest daughter slept.

The father had asked all his family to meet at his home for dinner. His oldest daughter did not arrive, and the others were eager to eat. He asked his youngest daughter to get her sister, and she ran to the small, clean home. She tried to pull open the blanket door, but there was something massive holding it down.

She ran to the window and, standing tall, peered into the home. All she could see were massive scales. Then she saw them move. The youngest daughter ran to her father and told him what she had seen. He gathered up his medicine pouch, two prayer sticks, cornmeal, and followed his youngest daughter. There in the window he saw the huge snake.

The father said, "I am your priest. I ask you to let my daughter leave. She is yours, but let her come to us for blessings before you take her."

The father's voice woke the oldest daughter. She saw the massive scales. She was so frightened she couldn't move. The father called out, "I am your priest. I ask you to let my daughter go. We shall have a ceremony for you."

The massive snake gathered up his coils. He could not move to speak. The father called out, "I am your priest. Let my daughter go. We know that you have won her. She needs a blessing before she leaves."

The snake coiled his neck up to the ceiling. He swallowed part of his tail. The father cried, "Your priest asks you to let his daughter come for a blessing." The snake lifted his tail into an arch, and the daughter crawled out on all fours and ran to her father. The father took the two prayer sticks and placed them in the door. He sprinkled cornmeal around the home. The medicine pouch remained in his hand.

The father took his daughters home, and the family listened quietly as he spoke. "You have done something which we have told you not to do, my daughter. You used the sacred spring. Since you love water and need water around you all day, it is perhaps for the best that you go with the sacred snake. Tomorrow, at dawn, you will begin the rest of your life with him. Tonight we shall have a blessing feast."

The oldest daughter was frightened. Her father sent the family to call the people of the village together. Meanwhile, Sacred Snake breathed in the air of Father Sky, and he lifted the massive body, placing it back in the sacred spring. There was much to do.

Next morning, the village was alive with excitement. Sacred Snake slowly slithered his massive scaled body out of the sacred spring. He ate the offerings of food. He took the prayer sticks. He slowly moved to the village. His giant head entered the village while the middle of his body was leaving the spring. It was not until midday that his tail coiled around him in the village.

The father started a chant. The people followed. The oldest daughter was brought out of her father's home. She wore a white manta, white moccasins, a headdress of feathers, and snake skins. Her face was painted with the colors of corn. She walked to Sacred Snake. Sacred Snake lifted his head onto her back.

The drums began to beat as the oldest daughter started her journey to the sacred spring, carrying Sacred Snake on her back. Sacred Snake's head was intensely heavy, and the daughter pulled strength from within her and tried to stand. She staggered and fell many times, but the strong body of Sacred Snake righted her on her path. She pulled through the day and into early night.

Sacred Snake's long body had hardly moved, and the daughter felt tired and frustrated. Darkness was now upon the land. The people had gone to their homes.

Sacred Snake breathed in the air of Father Sky. His long, scaly body shrank, and his heavy head changed form. The strong, handsome face of a brave warrior appeared. The scales gathered on the ground like a long blanket of silver; and a young man now walked beside the daughter, who continued to bend in her efforts. The brave warrior reached down and pulled up the long blanket of silver scales. He rolled it and placed it on his back, tying the blanket with a leather thong.

"Young maiden, why do you bend forward as one with a burden?" a man's voice echoed out to her in the dark night.

"Oh, I have such a load. I carry Sacred Snake, and he is so heavy I can but barely hold his head. His body is the length of four mountains and we have far to go. Could you help?" The oldest daughter did not turn.

"Beautiful maiden, I stand beside you and see that you are walking alone. There is no one on your back. There is no long body following. You are alone."

The oldest daughter lifted her hand to her shoulder, for she could feel the weight of the massive head. But nothing was there. She stopped and turned to see the long body that she was sure she felt. Nothing was there. Brother Moon lifted above the mountain and lit the dark night sky.

The oldest daughter stared into the face of the warrior. "Who are you? You are not from my village. Where is Sacred Snake?"

The brave warrior smiled. "I am Sacred Snake," he said. "I have decided to walk with you rather than have you carry me."

The eldest daughter stepped back. "You are not Sacred Snake! Sacred Snake is huge and heavy. You are not he!"

The brave warrior turned his back to her. "Here is my skin. I will carry it and give you a rest."

The oldest daughter sat down on the ground. "Will you let me return to my family? Will you let me go?"

The brave warrior knelt beside her. "No, I have admired you for a long time. Now that I have you, you are mine and I am yours. We shall live long. We shall have a good life. Come, let me help you."

The brave warrior carried the oldest daughter. They went to the sacred spring. Brother Moon hid behind a large, grey night cloud as Sacred Snake carried his maiden into the sacred spring water. They disappeared and were never seen again.

9. Greedy Brothers

At Soldier's Creek in Brule Sioux country there was a rattlesnake's hole. One rattlesnake, it was said, lived alone in the hole. The hole only had room for one tremendous body, its powerful smell, and the odor of greed that came from it. This one snake, it was said, came from the selfish greed of three brothers.

There were four brothers who left home in search of buffalo. They killed a strong buffalo out on the plains, and stood as four when the dead buffalo lifted its head and told them that they could eat of its meat, but that they must leave the skin, head, hooves, and tail in place.

The four agreed to do this. They skinned the buffalo and removed the meat. They pulled the tail straight out from the head and placed the hooves as they should be. They carried the meat not far from this buffalo corpse and proceeded to dry it, cook it, and cut it for carrying. The day was long and they were very hungry by nightfall.

The four brothers ate their fill, wrapping the rest of the meat carefully in leather to carry it back to their people. Then they slept apart from one another, which was unusual. The youngest brother noticed this, and saw his oldest brother scamper through the darkness to retrieve the skin and fur of the buffalo. He waited; then he saw his middle-older brother cautiously run back to get the tail and hooves of the buffalo. Then his middle-younger brother sneaked off in the night to bring back the head of the buffalo.

The youngest brother waited. He waited until all of his three brothers were asleep. Quiet as clouds in the night, he gathered up all the parts of the buffalo and took them back to the place where the animal had been skinned.

He laid them out as they should be. He joined them together and said a prayer of respect. When he looked up, there in front of him stood the buffalo. The fine, strong, whole buffalo lifted his nose in the air and bellowed. The youngest brother remained kneeling, watching the buffalo as it trotted away to greet the rising sun.

The youngest brother ran back to his brothers. He was eager to tell them of this wonder. When he entered camp, all was quiet. He sat and stared at the empty bedrolls. He called out for his brothers, but there was no one around. The youngest brother shook his head. He knew his brothers were greedy, but they had left all their belongings for him to carry home.

He knelt down and began to roll the bedrolls. As he moved the blanket, he heard a sound. It was a rattling. He jumped back. From out of his older brother's bedroll slithered a rattlesnake. From out of his middle-older brother's bedroll also slithered a rattlesnake, and from his middle-younger brother's slithered another rattlesnake. The youngest brother lifted his bedroll to find nothing.

The youngest brother studied the three snakes. They slithered in and out of the moccasins, the loincloths, the empty bedrolls. The youngest brother then knew that his brothers had turned into rattlesnakes. Their disrespect for the buffalo had brought them to this. The youngest brother unrolled the buffalo meat and left it out for the rattlesnakes. They did not harm him, and were hungry for the meat.

The youngest brother ran back to the people and told them of what had happened. When he returned with the people, all that remained of his three older brothers was one large rattlesnake that had burrowed into the ground and lay in its fat stupor alone.

The people do not bother this snake, and they are very respectful of the game they kill. When respect is given, respect is received.

Wolves

The Hudson Bay Eskimo think of the wolf as a poor woman who had so many children that she could not find enough for them to eat. They grew thin and weak and were changed into wolves that constantly roamed the land in search of food. The pain of the mother is said to be heard at night as she cries out.

*The Pueblo Indians were given the wolf as a gift by the mother creator **Ut'set**. She brought the people to this world in the far north through the **Shi-pa-pu**, place of emergence.*

*They traveled to the center of the earth, searching for the place of harmony and finding a location that was beautiful and filled with many plants. But the ground was wet, too wet for the people to walk upon. Ut'set called for the cougar and asked if he had any medicine to harden the road. He tried but could not harden the earth. Ut'set then sent out the bear and asked him to harden the earth. He tried but could not. Ut'set also sent out the badger, but he could not harden the wet land. Ut'set then asked the all-being creator **Sus'sistinnako**, who* told her to send out the wolf, the bear, the badger, and the shrew to use their medicines together to harden the earth.

Ut'set did this. The four of them were unable to harden the earth. Finally, a woman was sent from the Spider Society, and with the help of these four animals, she was able to make the earth hard enough for the people to stand, walk, and live upon.

The wolf holds great magic and more often than not is represented as a female. Wolf possesses the power of the night, the healing power of the spirits, and wisdom to instill courage.

The Cherokee have a hunting story that tells of the power of the wolf. If a hunter does not show respect to the animal he has killed, he will be haunted by one of the Spirit Guardians of the hunted. On the other hand, if a hunter shows respect and prays before and after killing an animal, the deer, the wolf, the fox, and the opossum will guard his feet against frostbite.

The Cherokee wolf is believed to be the watchdog and the side hunter for **Kana'ti**, the Power Spirit of game animals and insects. Among the Cheyenne an important clan was known as the **Ani'wa'ya**, Wolf People. They would never kill a wolf and believed that it was good luck to avoid the animal at all cost. They knew the spirit of the slain wolf would revenge his death.

The Kiowa referred to the Pawnee as the Wolf People because they had a peculiar style of shaving their heads, with two long scalp-locks hanging down from the sides. The word for Pawnee in the Kiowa language sounded like a wolf howling in victory or finishing the kill.

The wolf is known among the Isleta people as **K'y'jo'**, and the Tewa call it **ko'yo**, "grey wolf." For the Tewa People, it holds the power of the east, making it one of the zenith power-medicine animals. They throw it sacred cornmeal in ceremony. Though the grey wolf is now very scarce in New Mexico, its magic lives on through the myths.

1. Ghost Hunter

Some of the Dakota are fearful of wolves. Others know the honor of the wolves and perhaps remember the old stories. There once was a man who went out on a hunt. His family was hungry and desperate for food. He hunted alone—not the way of hunters. The Dakota had a tradition that hunters were to travel in groups; and if there was a lot of game, the many hunters would carry it to the village. Food was hunted, shared, and appreciated by all. That was the way of the people.

This man traveled alone in his hunt. He made camp near the place of the tall trees. He slept fitfully and awoke in the night to the sound of wailing. A ghost appeared before him, hovering in a long, white deerskin dress; white moccasins; and with long, white hair floating around her head. The ghost groaned and wailed in the voices of the hunter's woman and his children. Another ghost appeared, dressed as a man mourning for one who has died in disgrace. The hunter ran. He left behind his arrows, bows, and spear heads. He ran into the darkness. As he fled, he ran headlong into another ghost.

This was an older woman resembling his mother, and she was floating high in the air. She was dressed in white and cried white tears which fell down on top of him like snow. Her white hair blew around her as her form floated to the hunter. He fell to his knees, keeping his head down. The white ghost woman floated over him crying. The hunter did not move.

A howl filled the air. The white woman ghost shattered with the sound. The howl grew louder and louder. A man approached the hunter and then spoke to him. The hunter could not understand what the man was telling him. He watched the feet of the man walking around him as the man spoke. The feet moved round and round and round and round the hunter. The man spoke harshly, and the hunter closed his eyes. When he opened them, a wolf was pacing round and round and round and round him.

The wolf moved around the kneeling hunter. The wolf sniffed the hunter's moccasins. The wolf sniffed the hunter's face. The wolf sensed the hunter's fear. The hunter didn't move.

The night air was still, and Brother Moon was only half-way across the sky. The hunter had disobeyed the rules of his people. Ghosts were sent to kill him. The wolf lifted his jowls and grabbed the hunter's belt with his sharp, white teeth. The wolf growled, tugging on the belt, and the hunter stood and followed. The wolf let out a yelp. The hunter followed the wolf to another camp.

There were hunters from another tribe, and they needed another hunter. The wolf pulled the hunter to the ground and moved into the clearing near the others. As the wolf walked to the fire, his shape turned into that of a man. The man spoke with the others. They listened and nodded, smiling. The man turned and beckoned the hunter to enter the clearing and meet the others, which he did. As the hunters talked, the strange man stepped back into the forest. He returned to the shape of a wolf.

The wolf lifted his head and howled, disappearing in the night. The hunter was adopted into this group and was treated well. He became the best hunter of them all, and he never hunted alone. Whenever he returned from the hunt, he would leave meat outside the camp. In the morning the meat was gone, and there were only the paw prints of one lone wolf.

2. White Wolf Woman

The Zuni Indians tell of a raid that took place at night, long ago. The Navaho came in the night, riding fast horses, and stormed the Zuni village. A maiden was on her way back from a sick friend's home when she was swept up and carried off. The Navaho were known for quick raids and their use of slaves.

The maiden lay tied over the back of a galloping spotted horse. Her body hit against the strong muscles of this fast-moving horse. They traveled all night. At dawn, they arrived at a village. A Navaho woman helped the maiden off the horse and held her up as they went to a home. The Zuni maiden slept all day.

That night, the Navaho man came into his home. His woman was outside cooking over the fire. The Navaho man leaned over and began to pull on the maiden's clothes. The Navaho woman came with the food, took her bedroll, and went outside, leaving the man and maiden alone. It was a very long night.

The next evening came too soon. The Navaho man returned. He demanded his food. He pulled the Zuni maiden to him. She withdrew and went outside. The Zuni maiden spent the night outside. Before dawn the maiden awoke. Beside her stood the Navaho woman with a blanket, food wrapped in leather, and a small sealed basket of water. The Navaho woman pointed to the rising sun. The maiden ran, carrying the blanket, bundle, and basket. The day became warm, snow melted, and the winds were calm.

Strong legs ran quickly away from the sleeping Navaho village. The Zuni maiden ran through bushes, over stumps, and walked on sandy river beds, brushing over her footprints with a *chamisa* bush. She reached a high mesa and looked behind her. No one was following. No one had found her path. The wind blew against her soft, young face. Her large, piercing brown eyes stared out in wonder of where she was.

The wind reminded her of her hunger. She opened the bundle and found two pieces of jerky and two loaves of flat cornbread. She ate them all at once, for she was very hungry. She drank most of the water. Then she got up and continued to run—falling at last under a juniper tree. Frantically, she dug at the dirt, made herself a niche, and slept.

When she awoke, fear was strong in her eyes. Her thin, dirty fingers grabbed for the food. She realized that she had eaten it all. She lifted the sealed basket of water to her dirty, cracked lips and drank until there was not a drop. Her heart pounded in her chest. Her eyes darted around her, looking for trouble. There was none. She heard the wind blow over her. She felt the warmth of the sun. She saw a bush rolling in the wind. Her dirty, scratched legs leapt up for a fast run.

The evening sky came, and hunger filled every part of her being. Juniper berries were for healing or death, depending on the way they were used. She did not hold that knowledge. Rabbitbush was wind dried, but she could not eat that without fear of choking. The dead sage branches were buried by the wind. The sand was warm but provided no food. The earth beckoned to her. She curled up, falling asleep with the blanket wrapped around her small, hungry body.

The night wind brought a heavy snowfall. Snow fell on the blanket and soaked it. The cold, wet weight of the blanket made her colder. She kicked it off, and with cold legs and moccasins filled with snow, the maiden ran falling in the snow. Sleep took her.

A patter of paws came up to the sleeping figure. A long, furry white nose sniffed at the head of the maiden. Sharp, white teeth stained with blood shone out from under the thick, white-furred jowls. Silver-blue eyes turned up to the Great Spirits and called out in the night. A blood-curdling howl cut through the night like a knife.

The Zuni maiden sat up and tried to lift her arm, but it would not move. The white wolf loped away in the darkness. The maiden stared up into the night sky. The howl had awakened the stars. She prayed to the Great Spirits. She heard the sound of a growl, and then death echoing through the silent night air. The white wolf was illuminated by the moon reflecting off the snow. He dragged his kill to the maiden.

The dead animal was warm. The white wolf placed his heavy paw on the maiden's chest and pulled the dead animal over her frail, freezing body. The white wolf chewed on a lifeless, bloody leg and pulled it free to the maiden's mouth. She ate the raw leg meat, letting the blood fall on her chest.

The dead animal brought life to her body. Sun rose with all his splendor in the new light of day. The maiden's eyes watched as White Wolf turned and loped away. The earth was still. The dripping of snow off the trees reminded her of her flight. She pushed away the heavy carcass. Her hands were mixed with blood, snow, and dirt. Her face hardened with fear. She looked to the east. If her village was there, she would find it, or die. She shook her moccasins and tied them tightly to her blistered feet. Her head was held high as she ran, welcoming the guidance of Sun.

The winds came at midday, burning her cheeks and tangling her long, black hair around her neck. Her feet moved steadily, but her legs were chapped by the cold wind. She was determined to find her way back to her people. The chill of the night filled the air with ice. Her lungs burned. Her eyes could not stay open. Her hands felt the cold earth as she fell. She felt her spirit enter into her throat.

"No! No, I will find my way home. I will find my mother and my father. I will make it home!" She buried her tears in the snow. As strong as silence came the blood-piercing howl. Paws loped silently across the snow. A white nose sniffed in the night. A howl cut through the night once again. The silent movement of the white wolf could barely be seen in the cloudy, moonlit night. The white paws found the cold body shivering in the snow. The thick, white fur rubbed against the torn leather dress, and the maiden felt warm. They slept.

The two friends traveled for four more days. At dawn of the fifth day, the white wolf woke the maiden. There in the distance was her village. Her feet struggled over the rough terrain. She gasped as she saw the kiva ladders and the fields of her family. Next to her ran the panting white wolf. She called out with joy to the men on the roof. She called out, telling them her name and her joy at being home. The men watched.

They grabbed their arrows and pointed them at the maiden. She froze in her flight. The men told her to move away. They would kill the white wolf that chased her.

Her voice shattered the air. "No! No! This wolf brought me home. This wolf has given me my freedom. No, you must never hurt this white wolf!"

The men shook their heads and descended the ladders to the ground. She stood tall as they approached her. The white wolf was gone. The maiden fell to her knees.

They carried her home. They left her there on the cold, bare floor. They left her there. They left her there without a word. Lying on the floor next to her was her father. The maiden called to him. He did not respond. The winds of life had left his body long ago.

The home had bare walls, swept floors, naked wooden beams. The grinding stones, the bedrolls, the ceremonial baskets were gone. Tears filled her eyes. She had come home to an empty house of death. The maiden pulled strength from within her and told the people that she was not a traitor. The people would not talk to her. The people left her alone.

Yucca root was dug with bloody, worn fingers to make yucca soap. The tender love of a daughter washed the father's hair. The torn clothing, ashen moccasins, and solitary blanket dressed the father. His body was carefully pulled by his frail daughter. She pulled her father's body through the village.

The people watched. They said nothing. The father's body left its track as it was placed in the Cliff of Death. A piercing, soulful voice carried the chant of good journey; a prayer of peace was sent to the Great Spirits in the smoke of a simple fire; and cornmeal borrowed from other burial bowls was given to this father for his safe journey.

The empty house was home. Sometimes food was left at the door in the night. No one spoke to this one. Time brought age, age brought weakness, and it was time for her to leave the village and go to the place of death. Her heart knew that she would never be taken. She would have to go herself.

She washed her hair in yucca soap. She pulled her worn leather dress over her weak, bony body and tried to stand. She could not. Sliding along, she pulled her body out of the door to the path that led from her village. She lifted her head. This was her village, her "home."

The people stood aside. They watched her crawl. She pulled her frail body up the hill. Her eyes still held strength. She turned her head. A howl echoed out. A blood-curdling howl reverberated across the land. The howl of freedom flowed from her lips as her body changed into that of a white wolf. Her legs gained strength. Her eyes glowed silver-blue. She loped along the hills to her freedom.

There is a woman with white blowing hair that stands at the top of White Wolf Woman canyon today. She has been seen to change to a white wolf. Many who have lost their way find their home because of her. Her magic is her freedom.

3. Wolf-Chief's Son

The Tlingit tell of a time when starvation took many of their people. One young boy carried his bow and arrow with him everywhere he went. He was sure that he would come across something that he could hunt to feed his starving family.

One afternoon, he started back to his village. As he walked he heard a funny sound. He ran ahead and hid. He waited to see what was following him. There was nothing there. The boy continued walking, and soon he heard the sound again. The boy turned and caught a small animal.

It looked like a pup but was larger. The boy picked up the pup and carried it under his shoulder blanket. When he got home, he gave it to his mother, and she washed it for him. The boy took some red-dye paint and crushed it between his teeth. He then spit the paint on the pup and it stuck to the pup's fur.

The boy took the pup with him when he went into the woods. It ran off and returned with a grouse. The boy thanked the pup for finding food. He took the grouse home and his family ate well. The pup grew larger, stronger, and more aggressive. It became a wolf.

The next time they went hunting, the wolf found a mountain sheep. The boy was thankful and gave the wolf fat from the sheep. Every time the boy went hunting with the wolf, they found meat.

One day, the boy's older sister's husband asked if he could use the wolf for a hunt. The boy said that it was all right, only the wolf should get the best meat of the first animal killed. The older sister's husband agreed to this. They went hunting and the wolf killed a sheep. The man only gave the wolf the entrails of the sheep. The man yelled out to the people that the entrails were all that was worthy of this wolf. The wolf whined and ran away through the mountains.

The man returned with his meat. He was proud of the fine sheep he had gotten. When the boy asked where his wolf was, the man told him what had happened. The boy went to the place of the kill and saw the footprints and saw the red paint of the wolf. He followed the tracks. As he walked he had a vision. He knew that this wolf was really Wolf-Chief's son who had been sent to help the people.

The boy followed the trail for a long time. He came to a lake with a village on the other side. He heard people playing. He tried to see what they were doing, but he couldn't. Then he thought, "I wonder how I get over to those people."

As he thought this, smoke came out from under his feet. A door opened below him and he was told to enter into a subterranean chamber. An old woman met him. Her name was Woman-Always-Wondering. She asked him, "Son, why are you here?"

He answered, "Grandmother, I have lost my wolf which helped me and my people. I have come to find him."

The woman spoke. "Your wolf's people live across from here. The wolf you seek is Wolf-Chief's son. That is his father's village where they are playing and making so much noise."

The woman pointed under the lake. The boy asked, "Grandmother, how can I get there?"

The old woman looked into his eyes. Her words entered his mind without her lips moving. "My little canoe is below us. Before you get into it, shake it and it will become large enough to carry you."

The boy nodded his head, for he wanted her to know that he heard her thoughts. She continued, "Get inside the boat and stretch yourself on the bottom. Do not paddle. Tell it with your mind where you wish to go and it will take you there."

The boy did as he was told. The canoe landed on the other side of the lake. He got out and stood on the shore. Then the canoe became very tiny, and the boy put it in his pouch. He went to the boys who were playing. He watched them.

They were playing with a rainbow. He asked them if they knew the way to Wolf-Chief's house. They showed him. There was an evening fire next to Wolf-Chief's dwelling, and the boy crept up to the trees near the evening fire. He peered around to see what the people were doing. A wolf was playing while running around the fire.

The large Wolf-Chief walked out of the dwelling. He called out, "There is someone here looking at us." The little wolf ran to the boy and began to lick his face. Wolf-Chief came to the boy. "You were given my son to help your people when they were starving. Your people did not appreciate my son. My son will stay here with me." Wolf-Chief clapped his hands, and the little wolf ran to his father.

"Come, let us sit by the fire," he continued. The two of them went to the fire. Wolf-Chief sang a sad song, and the little wolf that was near them changed shape and became the same as the boy. He went over and sat by his friend. Wolf-Chief then told the boy, "You go to the wall and take out the fish-hawk's quill that is hanging on the wall." The boy did as he was told and returned.

Then Wolf-Chief said, "Whenever you meet a bear, hold the quill straight toward it and the quill will leave your hand." Wolf-Chief then reached into his pouch and pulled out a bundle. "This is for sickness. If there is someone who hates you, put the bundle on the left side of him and it will kill him. If someone is sick, put the bundle on the right side of him and it will cure him. Now eat this and go."

The boy ate the food, then went to the lake. He took the tiny canoe out of his pouch and it grew, so he sailed back to the place of the old woman. He thanked the grandmother and set out on his way home. As he walked through the forest, a large bear came after him. He held up the quill and it flew straight to the bear's heart.

He skinned the bear and gathered up the meat, then walked on until he saw a large herd of wild sheep. He lifted the quill and all the sheep fell over dead. He found the quill in the last sheep. He took what meat he could carry and hid the rest. He continued home. When he reached his village everyone lay dead. He realized that he had been gone a long time.

The boy took out the sacred bundle. He lifted it to the right side of all the people. When he lowered it again, all the people stood up alive. He went to the place where he hid the sheep and brought them all food. These people who were restored to life had very deep-set eyes.

Whenever anyone was sick, the boy had a cure. Whenever his people were threatened, he could protect them with his sacred bundle. The people always had food, and they prospered until the boy became a man, and the man an old one, and the old one died.

4. Three Mountain Wolf-Water Monster

The Chiricahua Apache tell a story of a woman who dressed in white buckskin. She was a very pretty woman who had been told by her father to go to the spring and get water. This spring is in the Three Sisters, or Tres Hermanas, Mountains. The pretty woman went to the spring.

The people waited for her to return. They were anxious for the water. But the woman did not come back. The people walked to the spring and looked for her. All they found was the water jar, and they saw her trail leading away from the spring and followed it. She had mysteriously walked up the path into the Three Sisters Mountains.

They followed her path as far as they could. Her footprints were marked on the cliff walls as if she had gone straight up the mountain. The people could not follow her, nor could they understand how the woman walked up the mountain in such a manner.

They walked around the mountain and hunted for her. They called on the medicine men to sing and pray for her to return. She did not. Finally, the people got together and talked about where the best medicine man could be found. Someone knew of a medicine man who was good at finding lost spirits.

He arrived and got all the people together. He sang and sang and sang and sang to find out where she was being held. As the sun rose on the fourth day, the medicine man stood and pointed at the mountains. "She is alive. She lives in the mountains. If we wish to find her, we must go up into the mountains."

The mountains gave the medicine man his power. He knew them and had a good idea where she was. Some of the people followed him, and he ordered them to wash their bodies in corn pollen. Every part of their body was to have corn pollen on it, or they would be in great danger. The people did as he said.

They climbed to a rock wall, and the medicine man sang. A place in the rock wall opened and a door appeared where there had been only solid rock. They entered a crowded room to find they were not alone. Standing around them were bears, mountain lions, badgers, moles, wolves, and wild fierce animals that they had never seen before.

The medicine man continued to sing. The people sang with him. The animals sang. Another rock wall opened in front of them. They entered a hall to find a bench of sand. It slowly lifted into the air over their heads to reveal a passageway. The medicine man stepped forward. He sang. Some people followed him along with the animals. They traveled a long distance. It was dark, crowded, and at times the animals growled. The medicine man continued to sing. The people continued to sing. The animals sang, too.

They came to another room filled with ferocious animals. They continued to sing. They waited for another door to open. The walls remained. They sang. They sang to each wall. The walls remained. They sang together. The walls remained. They continued to sing.

A large bear pushed his way to the medicine man. "The one that you search for is here. She is fine. She is the woman of the power spirit man who dwells here. You cannot go further." The medicine man continued to sing. The people continued to sing. The animals continued to sing. The wall opened to reveal a camp on top of the mountain.

There, in the early evening, was a camp with a fire burning in the center. The large bear walked toward the woman. As he moved to her, his body changed into that of a wolf. He sat down on his haunches next to the woman, and she greeted her visitors.

"I am glad to see you. This is where I am now. I cannot return with you, for I choose to stay here with my man. This place is of great beauty and holds the power of beauty within it. I cannot return. I shall send food to you, and keep you safe from harm, but I cannot return."

The people begged her to return with them. She told them no. The animals asked her to watch over them. She said, "If you choose to stay around this holy place, you will increase in number. I will always be with you. You will always have plenty of horses, food, and the enemy will not bother you. Keep the vision of this place in your spirit and all will be well with you."

The woman walked away. A rock wall came down. They had no choice but to return. They met the people in the first room and told them of what had happened. The medicine man left the people and returned to his place. The animals went their way. The people returned to the village.

The people had a meeting and decided that this was a great evil that had befallen them. They voted to leave and go back to Arizona. They packed up the village and traveled four days. On that fourth night they were all killed.

It is said that at night at the base of the Three Sisters Mountains, you can hear the cry of the wolf. The wolf, some say, is the power man who took the woman away. Some call him the wolf that changes into a protector. He is there, and he howls at night to remind the people of his woman's promise.

5. Wolf Star

The Pawnee creation spirits gathered together to create the Place where the people lived. The creation spirits were called together by the One, but the One forgot to call on Wolf Star Spirit. He found out about the great council meeting, and he was angry, blaming the trouble on *Paruksti*, the Storm of the West, whom the spirits sent out to inspect the people's Place to be sure of its completeness.

Paruksti carried the people in a whirlwind leather bag. Whenever he was tired, he would set the bag down and the people would come out, set up camp, and have a buffalo hunt. After Paruksti had rested, he would gather the people up in his leather bag and go on his way.

Wolf Star Spirit noticed this. He placed Wolf on the earth to follow Paruksti. One time when Paruksti was asleep with his head on the leather bag, Wolf came. Wolf gently pulled on the bag. He took the bag to the flat lands. The people came out, set up camp, and prepared to hunt for buffalo. Except there were no buffalo. They saw Wolf and invited him to eat their dried meat with them and share in stories.

Paruksti awoke. Frightened at the loss of his leather bag and the people, he hurried to the flat lands. When he saw Wolf, he chased him and told the people of Wolf's identity. The people pursued Wolf and killed him. Paruksti did not like this. He told the people that they would have to take Wolf's skin, dry it, make a sacred bundle of it, and always be known as the *Skidi*, or Wolf-People. Paruksti told the Great Spirits of what had happened. They met with the people, telling them that since they had brought death to the Place, they had also brought death to themselves.

The first dried Wolf skin lay on the ground near the sacred tent. Just before dawn, the sacred Wolf skin lifted from the ground. Some say that it turned back into the shape of Wolf and ran into the sky to become *Tskirixki-tiuhats,* or the Star of Wolf-He-Is-Deceived. It is said that it appears in the southeast just before the rising of the Morning Star. Wolf constellation deceives the wolves, who begin howling to greet the morning.

Those who had killed first Wolf became wolves. Now they run howling in their sorrow, only to be hunted themselves.

6. Wolf Woman Running

The Sioux warrior was cruel to his woman. He hit her if she was late with his food. He kicked her if she slept. He yelled at her when she was in childbirth for she was not caring for him. The Sioux warrior laughed at her in front of the others.

He would pull off her clothes and jeer at her in front of the men.

The cold wind blew across the dark sky. The dullness of the days magnified the anger that was inside this woman. Her children were now old enough to laugh at her. Her man had taken on another woman who was younger. The dark sky reflected the darkness in this warrior's woman. She had had enough.

The evening meal was being served. Her family was waiting for her to bring the food. Her fingers were burnt, disfigured from work, and her back ached from the burden. She kicked dirt into the fire. She kicked dirt into the corn stew. She knocked down the poles that held the cooking pots. She grabbed the buffalo hide that lay in the dirt. There was no looking back. She was gone.

Her warrior man yelled. Her children screamed out nasty names. The woman was not there to hear them. The other Sioux people walked around the dirty stew. They listened to the family inside yelling, screaming, and laughing. They left them alone.

The dullness of the evening sky lightened as the woman ran to the east. The buffalo robe was warm. Her stomach was full from tasting the delicious stew she had made. She felt good. Her back no longer hurt. Her fingers burned with strength. She ran into the billowing light snow.

The snow fell thicker as the night grew dark. The woman let the sounds that spoke within her head guide her. She ran up to the side of a rolling hill and crawled into a cave. The cave was dark. The floor was soft dirt. She lay down, pulling her buffalo robe around her, and fell asleep. She let her mind travel in her sleep. She did not have to wake up to duties. She did not have to please anyone but herself. She slept.

Something touched her arm. She lifted her head and peered out in the darkness. The silhouette of a wolf's head was all that she saw. She laid her head down and went back to sleep. A wet tongue moved across her cheek. Her eyes opened to find a soft, wet nose sniffing her face. She fell back into a deep sleep.

When she awoke, she was alone. All around her in the dimness of the cave were little round burrowing nests. Fur coated the nests. The cave smelled. She walked out to find thick snow blanketing the land. All around the entrance of the cave were wolf prints. The woman walked to a snow-bent tree. She pulled loose a branch which she used to sweep out the cave. She left the nests alone. She sat in the cave and waited.

The evening winds returned with snow. Howls echoed up and down the plains outside. The wolves returned. They brought with them fresh meat. They brought dried wood. The woman built a fire, cooked some of the meat, and watched the wolves. She stayed many days and each day the wolves allowed her to move closer to them. She brushed them with pieces of the broken bush. She sang to them and they were peaceful.

She lived with them through eight winters. The wolves provided for her through the winters and summers. They went out early to hunt, while she stayed in the cave and sewed, cooked, rested, or made herself leather clothing. She cooked meat for herself, dried meat to put away, and brushed and cared for the wolves. She grew strong. She learned wolf ways. She felt the power of the wolf within her. She decided that soon she would hunt with the wolves.

The wolves licked their fur after the morning meat. Then they loped out into the plains. The woman, on this day, pulled on her newly sewn moccasins and ran after them. The wolves were unaware of her presence until they surrounded a deer. They noticed she was there. They turned their attack on her. She let the strength of time give her the speed to get away. She outran them. She became Wolf Woman Running.

She lived alone out on the plains for four days. She saw a pack of wild horses running. She made a simple spear and ran to the horses headlong. She was fast as she darted among them. She didn't see the other horses. They were galloping towards her from the west. They were mounted with Sioux warriors who were in search of ponies.

Wolf Woman Running sighted the wild pony she wanted. She lifted her spear, ready to throw, when something grabbed her arm. She was thrown across a moving horse that held a strong man. She shrieked in terror. She bit, kicked, fought this man. He was stronger. He held her firmly. He took her back to her Sioux family.

The women took her to the river and washed her. She fought them. They combed her snarled hair. She sat sternly. They tried to get her to speak. She was silent. The women took her to her warrior. She spat on him. When he tried to touch her, she bit him, drawing blood. They put her by herself.

Time passed. She began to sing the song of the wolves. Wolf Woman Running howled at the moon. She knew when people were going to be ill. She brought them medicine and showed them what to do without speaking. She talked with her hands. The people realized that she held great magic.

Chief White Buffalo called a meeting. He said that it was time to test the powers of those in the tribe. He wanted to have a testing with White Wolf Running. The old ones approved. Chief White Buffalo stood facing Wolf Woman Running and the tribe's other medicine woman. He opened his hand. Faster than thought he threw something at the two women. It was a white worm, and it entered into them before they could call it away. It entered into their spirits and began to gnaw inside them.

Chief White Buffalo clapped his hands four times and called the white worms back to him. They flew through the women's bodies to the magic hands of Chief White Buffalo. The women were so sickly they couldn't stand. Chief White Buffalo told them that they had magic but needed to learn more. In time, Wolf Woman Running became healthy and wise.

Wolf Woman Running remained with her people. She healed many before she died. She never spoke to or lived with another.

7. Medicine Wolf

The Blackfeet were moving camp when they were attacked by the Crow Indians, who had set a trap for them. The Blackfeet usually traveled slowly in a long line. The old men and the women were in the middle with the children in front of them. The warriors were in the front and the rear. The women were all along the line helping where they could.

The Crows rushed out, attacking the middle portion of the line of people. The Blackfoot warriors could not reach their children and women soon enough and many were killed. Others were taken prisoner.

One of the women captured was called Sits-By-The-Door. She was shoved ahead of the Crow warriors, who were riding horses, and ordered to run and keep up or die. She wearily ran with them to the Crow camp on the Yellowstone River. She was pushed in with other prisoners who were then divided among the Crow warriors.

Sits-By-The-Door went to a Crow who gave her to the keeping of his woman. Every night, the warrior would tie her feet together so that she could not escape. He also tied a rope around her waist and attached it to his woman, who was much older than Sits-By-The-Door. The Crow woman did not show any kindness or care for the young prisoner.

As the spring weather improved, the Crow men went out on more raids. Sits-By-The-Door stayed with the Crow woman, and each night the older woman would tie her up and they would wait for the return of the warrior. As time moved on, and the Crow warriors were delayed, the older woman began to teach Sits-By-The-Door how to speak the language of the the Crow. The two women began to share their lives and tried to help each other with the duties.

The Crow warrior returned. He watched as his dutiful woman tied up Sits-By-The-Door. The Crow woman listened to her man as he spoke about the raids that had taken place. The warriors had not found enough food, and the tribes that they had raided were in worse condition than the Crow. The food shortage was already hurting the people, and the migrations had not brought in any game. They would need to trade prisoners for food.

The Crow woman heard the men talking about trading Sits-By-The-Door for food. That night, she waited until her man was sleeping soundly. She untied Sits-By-The-Door, gave her food, moccasins, flint, and jerky, and told her the fastest trail out of the Crow camp.

Sits-By-The-Door escaped. She traveled all night. At daybreak, she hid in some bushes. The Crow discovered her absence and they started their search, for she was valuable to them. She was food for their children and warmth for the winter. They desperately searched the land for Sits-By-The-Door, but she had burrowed into the side of a small hill. Bushes blocked her view, as well as the Crows' ability to find her. Sits-By-The-Door stayed there for two days. She could hear the men walking next to her. She could hear the children crying out in hunger. She felt her heart beat in her chest as she heard her Crow captor calling out her name.

The fourth morning, the Crow packed up their belongings and moved. Sits-By-The-Door dug out of her hiding place and followed the movement of the sun. She hid in the daytime and ran at night. Soon, she was out of food, her moccasins were worn, and she was exhausted. She knew that if she did not find food she would die.

Early one evening, Sits-By-The-Door decided that she would start on her journey before dark and rest when she was tired. Perhaps she could find water, and if there was water, there was bound to be food. She lifted her dirty, weak body out of her hiding place and started to limp forward. Her hands were crusted with blood from digging trenches. Her feet were torn and crusty from walking over cactus and sharp rocks in the night. Her dress was ripped and caked with dirt, but her sparkling eyes held the hope of getting home.

She stumbled, her mind muddled as to direction, then straightened herself and heard something wheeze behind her. Sits-By-The-Door turned. Walking towards her was a huge, grey-brown wolf that was hot, breathing with difficulty, and limping. The wolf staggered to her and fell at her feet.

Sits-By-The-Door studied the wolf. His paws were bloody raw. His ribs were sticking out, and his tongue was dry. She carefully lifted the limp wolf; and with what little strength she had, she carried it on her journey. The full moon shone over their heads, and she decided to follow the direction of the wolf—toward the moon. Her path turned from where she knew her people were to the shadows of the moon.

She found a stream. She carefully laid the grey-brown wolf on the soft dirt. The wolf was gasping for air. He was trying to lick his nose with his dry tongue. Sits-By-The-Door cupped her hands as she gathered up water from the stream. She poured water on the wolf. There were sweet berries in the bushes, and she tasted them and spit the juice into the wolf's mouth. The wolf shivered in the cold night air. Sits-By-The-Door pulled him to her and wrapped her frail, thin body around him for warmth. They stayed the night, and the next day at the stream the wolf healed quickly. Sits-By-The-Door rested.

"Wolf," she said, "you have been given strength, food, and care. It is time for me to leave you to your own path. I must go home. For I cannot live out here and I need to be with my family. May you find your family."

She left the wolf at the stream. She walked all night until she could not walk anymore. She stumbled and fell. She rolled over on her back and studied the stars. Each had a name among her people. The stars were guardians, and each guardian was watchful. Sits-By-The-Door opened her mouth to say a prayer. "May this journey be good, may this journey be swift, and may there be peace and goodness in the next world."

Sits-By-The-Door let her eyes close as she waited for her spiritual passage.

"*Grrr, grrr, grrr.*" Grey-white fur lips curled as hackles were lifted. White, bloody teeth ripped meat from the bone. Sharp claws tore at the skin as the bloody chin nuzzled Sits-By-The-Door. Loud growling echoed in the night as the grey-brown wolf dragged a newly killed buffalo calf to the woman. The wolf barked. Sits-By-The-Door did not move. Next to her a transformation occurred.

A muscular hand reached into Sits-By-The-Door's torn pocket. The flint that the Crow woman had given her was used to build a fire. Water was poured into Sits-By-The-Door's parched mouth. Strong arms lifted the weak woman. She was placed nearer the fire. The killed buffalo calf was lifted to cook over the fire. Long, grey-brown hair blew around a stocky face. The elongated jaw wailed out a song that filled the night. Silver-blue eyes darted from the cooking meat to the sleeping Sits-By-The-Door.

The moon shone briefly between the passing clouds. Sits-By-The-Door moaned as the clouds separated her from the stars. She turned her face to look at the fire. Her head hurt, her neck was stiff, her fingers throbbed in pain, and sleep overtook her. The meat cooked slowly. A mud mixture was rubbed on her calloused feet. Sage, rabbitbush, and saltbush were quietly ground, mixed with water, and softly rubbed onto her arms, hands, neck, and face. The strong, short fingers moved magic medicine across the tired, weak spirit of Sits-By-The-Door.

The pink sky of early dawn covered the new day. Sits-By-The-Door heard the howl of a wolf. She sat up ready to run. There in front of her lay the cooked meat. Next to the meat sat the grey-brown wolf. The silver-blue eyes smiled at her.

"You have brought me food? Cooked food?" she asked, grabbing for the meat and ripping off a piece. "This is good. You are welcome to help eat this." The grey-brown wolf lifted up a piece of meat in his mouth. Sits-By-The-Door rubbed the back of her neck. She felt a powdery substance. She rubbed her fingers together and smelled them. "Sage, saltbush, and rabbitbush! How did this get on my neck?" Sits-By-The-Door rubbed the powder on her lips. "My mouth has been rubbed with fat grease. Did you know that, Wolf? Did you know that someone put fat grease on these lips?"

Sits-By-The-Door dried some of the meat the next day. Again that evening, she continued on her way home. The wolf followed her and provided food for her when she became hungry. After a time, they came to the Blackfeet camp. Sits-By-The-Door led the wolf dog into her lodge. She told her family and friends of her capture, her travel, and her friend the wolf. The wolf did not stay, but disappeared mysteriously the next evening. Sits-By-The-Door lived for four days with her people before she became deathly ill and died.

The following morning the wolf came to her lodge. It barked for food and was fed by her family and friends. Then one day, the wolf disappeared and was never seen again.

8. Wolf Daughter

There was a strong Eskimo family that lived near the water. The summer had been bleak and there was very little food. The mother called to her daughter. "You must go and marry the otter. He will be the one who shall save our family from starvation." The daughter listened to her wise mother. She took her bedroll and walked out on the ice. There she found a hole and called down into it, "Otter, I am here. I am your woman. Come to me!" There was no response.

The daughter waited, and every now and then she would call down into the hole. A head popped up from another hole further along. "You cannot be my woman, for my woman is strong and has teeth and thick fur. My woman can live in the water as well as on land." The otter disappeared. The daughter went home to her wise mother.

The wise mother thought on what her daughter said. She knew that there had to be a way to get her daughter to marry the otter. The mother sang songs, chanted, and practiced medicine all night. In the morning, she went to her daughter, who was now a white wolf. "Go, my daughter," she said. "Go and marry the otter."

The wolf went to the otter. He sat in the water with his head sticking out of the hole in the ice. "I am here, my husband," she said. "I have come to be with you." The wolf sat down near the otter. The otter shook his head. "You cannot live in the water. What kind of a wife will you be? You cannot come in the water and be with me!"

The wolf spoke softly. "You can live on the land as well as in the water. You come here to me." The otter dove into the water and disappeared.

The wolf sat back and began to howl dismally. The wind began to blow and the snow drifted along the ice. The snow fell into the otter's breathing holes and filled them with slush. Soon the holes were frozen over with ice—all of them, that is, except for the one where the wolf was sitting. This hole was kept clear of snow and ice. The wolf heard the otter going to each hole gasping for breath. Soon he came out of the one near where the wolf was sitting, and she could hear him sucking air.

The otter, nearly exhausted, came up to the surface. He crept out of the water and rolled himself in the dry snow. He shook off the moisture and stared at the wolf. "I will live with you. I will live with you."

"It is good that you have seen what is best," said the wolf. Then the otter asked her, "Have you some string or line? Give it to me and I will go and catch some fish for you and we can prepare a tent." The wolf gave him a piece of fishing line.

The otter went down into the hole and was gone for a time. Meanwhile, the wolf made a tent. The otter came back with a long string of fish. He left them in the ice hole, fastening one end of the string to the tent. The otter rolled in the snow to remove the water from his fur. He went to the tent and told his woman to go and get the fish that were in the hole in the ice. The wolf was so hungry, and there were so many fish, that she ate almost all of them.

The otter was fast asleep when she returned. She cleaned the rest of the fish and put them in a large kettle to boil for supper. She crept into bed with her man and the next morning she delivered a young otter and a young wolf. The father and mother sat down to eat with their children. The wolf hung her head in sorrow.

"What is it? Why is my woman sad?" Otter was seriously concerned. Wolf answered, "I wish I had some deer skins. I could make clothing for our children." The otter said, "Open the door and I will show you where I get the deer." It was early, and the otter went on his way to find the deer. Soon he saw a band of thirty, and since he had no gun to kill them, he frightened them. As they ran, he would spring up and land on their backs, biting at their spines. This killed them quickly.

After each kill, he would roll over and over and over and over in the snow to cleanse himself. After he had killed all the deer, he pushed them into a snow pile and left them there. He hurried home and told his wife that in the morning they would go and retrieve the killed deer. The wife had a big pot of fish cooked for his dinner that night. After eating, the otter went to sleep.

As soon as Otter was asleep, Wolf went out after the deer. She pulled four at a time near the tent, carefully placing them where they would be safe. That morning, the otter woke his woman. "It is time to carry the deer. Wake up and let's get to work." The wolf groaned, "I have already brought the deer while you were sleeping."

Otter was dumbfounded. He looked out the door and there were all the deer. Otter and Wolf skinned the deer. The wolf told her husband to make a scaffold for hanging the skins to dry. They did this quickly. The wolf was very talkative. They went to bed knowing they had done a good job.

Next morning, the wolf hung her head. Otter said, "Oh, no, what is it that you need now?" Wolf began to sniff. "I am thinking of my poor brothers and sisters who are starving to death. We have meat and they have nothing." Otter looked at Wolf. "What can we do to help them?"

Wolf pointed to the lake. "I told them that if they saw a large pile of ice on the lake, they would know that I was alive and that there was food for them nearby." Otter shook his fur. He went out to the lake and worked all day building up a mountain of ice.

On a hilltop nearby, a young boy stood looking down on the pile of ice. He called to his mother, for he had never seen anything like this ice mountain before. His mother slowly climbed up the hill to see what he wanted. She was weak from hunger and her bones hurt in the cold.

"Your sister, your sister is alive and she has food for us. Call your brothers and sisters. Find your father. There is hope. There is food!" The mother was most anxious to see her daughter again. The family gathered to go down to the ice and have food. The mother told them that they would have to go in the morning. She gave them each a special drink to swallow, and all night she sang, chanted, and prayed as their transformation began.

In the morning, the family appeared as wolves. They loped down the hill to the ice on the lake. There, Otter and Wolf were waiting for them, and they brought the family to their tent and gave them deer meat. They fell asleep when they were full. The next morning, Otter turned to his woman. She had borne him two more children. They now had two wolf children and two otter children.

Otter said to his woman, "Your brothers are greedy and they will make a fool of me."

Wolf woman shook her head. "No, they are grateful for what we have done. They will not do anything to hurt you." Otter shook his head. That day it was decided that the wolf brothers would hunt with Otter. The wolves ran after the deer, barking and scaring them. Otter waited until the deer were far from the wolves, and then he sprang on the backs of the deer and killed them. He rolled in the snow to clean his fur and mouth, gave his thanks to the deer spirit, and started home with his kill. Otter took a long time to drag four deer home.

He got there late after the wolves had returned with their one deer. Wolf woman had waited for her man before she ate. But the other wolves had eaten, and when otter brought his deer, they wanted more meat. Otter finally rested. The wolf brothers spoke loudly to their sister. "Wolf sister, did you notice how your otter's teeth and mouth are white? He did not kill these deer. He took ours!"

Otter got up from his resting place. He reached over and took his two otter children. He carried them carefully in his paws. "Wolf woman, I told you that your brothers would make a fool of me." Otter carried his two otter children into an ice hole. They jumped in and disappeared, never to be seen again.

Bears

The Tanoan word **Ke'** *is bear, and the Bear Clan traditionally was one of the largest in the Pueblo social groups. It was made up mostly of women who were the guardians of their pueblos. They monitored all that went on between women and men, and their permission had to be sought for a couple to marry. The* **Cacique,** *or census-taker, worked with the Bear Clan on the development of ceremonies and worship.*

Bears would appear to people in dreams and guide them through vision quests to a place where they would be safe from harm. The bears were believed to have once been people who decided to separate from the killers of animals and start their own group. The people who continued to hunt eventually killed off all the game and were starving. The Bear People came out of the forests and offered themselves as food, having the magic to turn their bodies back into bears if hunters left the skin and bones behind untouched.

There is a Hiniati ceremony performed when a young man kills his first bear. The first person to touch the animal becomes

a *honawai'aiti*, *or high acting member of a clan. The sacred
words used in honoring the bear are difficult to translate into
English. But to illustrate the ultimate respect people hold for
the bear, it might be helpful to review the terms. The skinning
and cutting of the bear meat is the called* **dickama**, *a word
parallel to the most sacred female food source known to the
people, cornhusk. The meat of the bear is referred to as* **kinati**,
*which is also the first female food source—a fresh ear of corn.
There are very few sexual distinctions in the Puebloan languages, for the sacred spirits of male and female are equal.*

*The first male was the germinator of life and is given
ultimate respect. The first female was the reproducer of life and
holds equal power. The corn seed is planted by the males, for
they place the seed into the spirit of Earth Woman. She, in turn,
listens to their songs, feels their nurturing tenderness, and gives
life to the seed. The corn grows within her to feed the men and
their families. Corn holds the highest fetish respect in
ceremony, and an ear of corn embodies the female concept
itself. Bear meat is the male counterpart of the female concept
and is of great importance in the mythology of Pueblo Indian
people.*

*A bear that has lived long and has not attacked or hurt
people is known as* **Ke'sen'doh**, *or Great White Grandfather
Bear.*

*The power of the bear is used in the most sacred of healings
and vision quests. The Pueblo curing ceremony takes four days
to perform, and the medicine society spends four days preparing for it unless the patient is critically ill, in which case the
members start work immediately. The fourth day of the
ceremony, the sick one is taken to the inner chamber of the
healing house. The healing ones have their sand paintings
placed on the floor along with their paraphernalia—bowls of
healing cornmeal, fetishes, flint knives,* **iarikos** *(corn fetishes),
and bear paws. A* **gaotcanyi** *(guard) watches the door to be
sure no one interrupts the curing ceremony.*

*The healing ones sit singing behind the altar as the patient is brought in and placed next to the wall, in front of the sand painting. The Wisest Healer of the men is called **Masewi**, or the Leader, and he sits to the left of the patient—the side of the spirit world. The Follower is called **Oyoyewi**, and he is the taker-away of pain and illness. He sits on the right side of the patient, whose close relatives stay at the end of the room praying quietly.*

*The healing ones sing and ask the spirits of the animals **tcaianyi** (Bear, Mountain Lion, Badger, Wolf, Eagle, and Shrew) to come into the chamber, traveling over the road of sacred cornmeal that has been prepared and laid out in front of the patient. The healing ones work only with sacred spirit power received from these animals. Next, one of the powerful healing women brings in a bowl of water, and the other healings ones place it near the altar. Then **Masewi** pours six dippers of water, and the animals are called to come and take from it.*

*The healing ones sing. **Masewi** takes powdered herbs from his bearskin bag and puts them into the water. The family leaves quietly, and only the strongest healing ones are left inside to work with the healing herbs. It is believed that people cured in this manner will have a bear come into their dreams and warn them of danger, or tell them of a better path to take in their lives. In fact, the bear is a guardian, and the sacred **ma-cinyi** (skin of bear's forelegs) and bear claw necklaces bring vision to those in need. As the stories themselves reveal, bears hold much respect.*

1. The Boy and the Bear

The Iroquois Cattaraugus Reservation holds a story about a grandson of a corn planter. There was a party out hunting a long way from home. As they gathered up their game to return, they noticed that a young boy being trained as a hunter was missing. The search lasted for two days and there was no sight of him. The cold winds came. Finally, the hunters left food and blankets for the young boy and returned home. They had just left when he entered the camp, and he cried for his parents. There was no answer. He sat huddled in the blankets, quietly crying.

A large, knowledgeable female bear came out of her cave. She cocked her head and listened. Somewhere below her was a human child crying. The mother bear went back inside her cave to find her cubs asleep. She ambled toward the crying boy, then hid. This mother was a very kind-hearted bear and thought, "If I help as a bear, he will either be frightened or try to kill me."

So the mother bear changed shape into that of a woman without clothes. She walked out from behind some rocks to the boy, and he was relieved to find someone who could care for him. The woman lifted the boy and took him to her cave.

The boy clung to her arms and breasts. He could hear sounds of bears and was frightened. Once inside the cave, he saw many young cubs playing. The boy cried, climbed down her, and took hold of her hand as he moved behind her. As he stood watching the cubs, he felt the shape of the woman change. There, next to him, was a large mother bear.

The mother bear spoke. "These are my other cubs. Now that you know the kindness of bears, you must respect them. Teach the others to leave bears alone." The boy stayed, learning bear ways and the magic of their power. He stayed with the bears until he was older, stronger, and more knowledgeable.

One fall day, the mother bear changed back into a woman. The boy was now a young man. He made her a simple covering, and she took him back to the village. His mother and father were glad to have him home with them. The young man grew into a fine hunter who never shot a bear. He grew strong and married a woman who also was trained with the knowledge of hunting. His woman traveled with him when he hunted.

She grew full with life and gave birth to a son—a boy she took along when they went on the hunt. The woman grew full with life again. She was loyal to her man, and when he went out, she insisted on going with him. On this occasion, the heaviness of the life to come slowed her, so she lay down on some soft leaves and waited for the hunting party to return. They did not. She sent her older son to the top of a hill to cry out for help. Her older son did not return.

The blood of life flowed from her body, and she gave birth to another son. She knew of certain ceremonies to perform, but she was alone and weak. She nursed her baby. "Oh, little one, you should know your father. You should know the name-givers! You are here with me and we are alone. If we sing, perhaps they will come." She sang to the sky until she was exhausted. They slept.

"Little one, your mother must eat. There is no warm cornmeal here. If I do not eat, your milk will be filled with evil spirits. The pure cornmeal of our people is far from here. I shall find us something to eat. You rest here under this tall cottonwood." She picked up her arrows and a bow.

The cub bear's tracks were easy to follow, and the killing was painless. She cleaned it and dragged it back to cook. She started a fire. The baby nursed as she cooked the meat. The woman felt weak, tired, and confused. No one came. She chewed the cooked bear cub meat until it was soft and then pushed it into her baby's mouth.

Her man found his older son, but the boy could not remember how far he had traveled. He sat and cried. His father lifted him up and followed his footprints. There were places were the ground was hard and no tracks could be found. His father continued searching. Before the sun set, he saw smoke on the horizon. He pushed his son to his back and ran to the smoke.

The father found his woman with the baby. "Woman," he said," are you here alone out in the dark?"

"I felt the waters of life leave me," she said. "Look, you have another son."

The father took his new son in his strong arms. "You had an easy birth. Did you name him yet?"

"No, for I was alone. There was no one here to help me with his name. There was no cornmeal for me to wash him in, or feed him, or for me to eat. We were hungry." She pulled a large piece of the bear meat off one of the sticks and began to chew on it.

"You found meat? Where did you find a deer? We walked up to the foothills to kill our deer. Were there deer down here?" The father handed his son back to his woman as she placed the chewed meat into the baby's mouth.

"This is not deer. This is bear cub meat. We had to eat something, and this was all that there was."

He stood. His eyes opened wide and glared at her in the firelight. "You never kill a bear! It is against our ways! You must leave. It is evil to kill a bear!"

He turned and lifted her up off the ground. The sound that came from his throat was frightening. He lifted her high in the air, and with all the strength in his body he threw her hard against the ground. Her weak body found its way to a stand. She did not turn, and she did not look back. She ran away into the night.

The father reached down to his baby son. "You shall be called He Who Eats Bear. You are not of my spirit."

The father pulled the baby closer to him. The infant was not breathing, and his face was white. The father took his dead baby son to the broken tree on the hill. The small, white body lay across the soft trunk dust. The father tore his hair. "This is not of his spirit. *EEEE-ah, EEEEE-ah!* Oh, Spirits, hear my song! This is not of his spirit!" The father washed his body in ashes and chanted all night.

Four days later, he built a shelter on the low land. The father lived with his older son in this humble home for two years. He asked for forgiveness every day. One morning, the older son came to his father and told him of the footprints. He told of how his bow and arrows were missing.

"Father, there are human footprints outside the meat-drying shed. Sometimes small bear prints follow these. I did not want to bother you with this, except that today my bow is missing and four of my best arrows. The small footprints go right up to my door and then leave. Who do you think took my bow and arrows?"

The father studied his son's face. "Small footprints? Are you sure that they are human?"

"Father, they are human. They are barefoot. The footprints have been coming here since the spring, but they never took anything before this."

They went outside and studied the prints. Some were bear tracks. The bears were small. The human prints were not much bigger, and they went straight up to the meat-drying shed, back to the door of the home, and then to the hill. The man and his son followed the tracks and came to the broken tree. There, in the tree, sat a small boy playing with the bow and arrows. He sat up on his knees, and, raising the bow overhead, he growled.

The father cautiously walked up to his small son. "You are alive. The spirits heard the song. You are alive!"

The small boy jumped out of the tree and ran to a cave. The father followed him. There, in the cave, sat the boy in the lap of a large mother bear. The small boy hugged the mother bear. He growled and bared his teeth as he suckled her breast. The father knelt near the opening of the cave. "That is my son you have there," he said.

The mother bear studied the father, then changed into a woman. "I have your small boy here with me," she answered, "for my small cub was taken by your woman."

The father hung his head in remorse. "That was not right. The spirits punished us for this evil deed. Your cub was not meant to die. It was an evil deed that killed him. I am most sorry."

The woman clicked her tongue. "You left your baby in the tree, thinking he was dead. He had choked on my cub's body." The woman took the small boy and gave him to his father.

"You may take him now, for he must learn of your ways. His spirit is with you. I will go back to my people." The woman walked slowly out of the cave.

The father took hold of her arm. "Wait. Your care has given life to my son. Your kindness has kept him from harm. Your ways will not be forgotten. You may stay with us, if that is the way."

Her long, white fingers stroked the young boy's cheek. "He is yours now," she said. "He has always been yours. It is time for me to return to my people and teach them what was taught to me by your son. You shall have your son to teach you."

She changed into a bear. The small boy screeched out his pain as she walked away from him. The boy tore at his father's chest with his long nails. He kicked and screamed as the mother that he knew left him in the strong arms of his father.

This one grew in his strength and taught the people to respect the bears.

2. Bear-Mother

The Haida tell of a chief's daughter of the Wolf Clan. Her name was Rhpis'unt, and she was very spoiled, proud, and bossy. She did not like to do anything that anyone else did. She perferred to live life in her own perfect manner.

One day she went out to pick berries with two of her less-than-perfect friends. They had chosen an area where there obviously were no berries at all. This chief's daughter walked down a path away from her friends who were less than perfect. Obviously they were too stupid to find the right berries! Rhpis'unt, in her most proper manner, stepped in something that was goopy and stank. She stopped to remove this disgusting matter from her delicate foot. It was smelly old bear dung! This was terribly disgusting! She shook her head as she removed the stinky matter from her foot.

"This bear was a dirty, filthy animal. I should have stepped in something that was not of great importance! Humpf!" Rhpis'unt then went on her most important way.

Rhpis'unt's clarity of thought had been muddled by this smelly imposition, and somehow she walked into a part of the forest that she did not know. There were berries all along the way and she soon filled her basket. Then it broke a strap and berries spilled all over the ground. Some even got dirty. "That dirty bear has ruined my berries," she complained. "He should leave his dung for someone less perfect!"

Rhpis'unt grew angrier and angrier at the bears. She grew tired and called out to her less-than-perfect friends. They did not answer. She tried to carry her basket, but it kept slipping. She lifted the basket to her shoulder, but it fell. She took the basket and the broken strap and placed it around her arm, but it flipped backwards. She sat down to collect herself and her berries.

Two men came walking through the forest. They greeted her with great respect. They were tall, heavy-boned, muscular, and had thick heads of hair. The men spoke to her. "Let us help you carry your broken basket. You should not tire yourself."

Rhpis'unt accepted their polite offer. They took the basket, helped her to her feet, and led the way. Rhpis'unt, the chief's daughter, quickly told them of her importance and of the fine berries she had collected. She followed the man in front of her and directed the one behind her around each stone or bush. She chattered about her family, her village, and her trouble with the dirty bear dung.

The trail was good. There was no need to be worried. They arrived at a village. Rhpis'unt stopped. She did not know this place. The people would not know of her importance. Rhpis'unt became quiet and followed the men. The leader took her to a house. He said, "I will see if my father is here. He would like to meet you." She waited, hearing two men talking.

"Did you find what you were seeking?"

"Yes, she is outside waiting to meet you."

"Bring her in. We shouldn't keep her waiting. I want to meet my new daughter-in-law."

She was led to a room with a huge man sitting on a blanket. Next to him was a large woman. Her eyes were closed and she was breathing deeply. Bearskin coats hung on the walls. Bearskin coats were stacked in piles on the floor. Bearskin coats were hanging over the window openings.

The huge man called to Rhpis'unt, "Come sit here by me. I want to see what you look like."

Rhpis'unt walked over to the huge man and sat on a bearskin blanket. He studied her face and said, "I will make arrangements for the union to take place." The huge man turned to talk to his son.

Rhpis'unt looked down. There, on her blanket, was a tiny, little woman who said, "I am Mouse-Woman. If you have any wool or animal fat, please give it to me right away. These can be used to help you get out of here. Hurry!"

Rhpis'unt pulled her woolen earrings off and some woven decorations from her hair, and she gave them to the tiny woman. She took some of the goat fat that she used to keep her skin soft and handed it to her as well.

Mouse-Woman told Rhpis'unt, "The Bear-People are angry with you for stepping in their dung. Then you insulted them. Bear-Chief is angry and he will bring you great pain. If you go outside to relieve yourself, dig a hole to hide your waste. Cover it with dirt and make a mound. Then put a piece of your copper bracelet on top of the mound. Always be careful, for you will be watched all the time." Mouse-Woman disappeared.

Bear-Chief called all the bears to come to a celebration that night to meet his daughter-in-law. Rhpis'unt asked if she could go out to relieve herself. She dug a hole behind the bushes. She covered it, then she broke off a piece of copper from one of her bracelets and placed it on top of the mound.

The bears who had been spying on her found the copper. They were astonished. They took it to Bear-Chief. "She is angry at our dung, for when she relieves herself she leaves copper behind!"

Guests began to arrive, and the chief talked with them. Then Bear-Chief's wife finally awoke. She pulled herself upright, calling to her man, "Why are there so many humans here?" He did not answer her but kept on talking to one of the guests. The wife growled, baring her teeth and showing her ugly body.

The firmness of that body was impressive. Her rolls of muscle rippled as she walked to the food. Her breasts sagged, banging against her large abdomen. Her breasts were human heads that were alive and moved. The light from her eyes showed the underworld house and all its forms of life.

Bear-Chief called attention to Rhpis'unt. "This is my daughter-in-law. If you see her in trouble, help her. She will bear the grandchildren of the Bear-People." Rhpis'unt gasped. She was beautiful, perfect, and the daughter of a great chief. She was not going to sleep with a bear, much less have his children. Rhpis'unt tried to find a way out of the large room, but there were guards at every door.

A drum sounded and great bowls of mountain goat fat were brought in and distributed to everyone. Bear-Chief announced that the goat fat was a gift to them from Rhpis'unt. This had been made through the magic of Mouse-Woman. The bears were grateful for the fat.

The young man who had led her to this place turned into a bear, picked her up, and carried her to his home. Rhpis'unt was now married to a bear. She learned that bears only used wet wood to start fires, and that they never went outside without their bear coats. When they put them on, they behaved like bears.

Sometimes her bear friends did not return, and when she asked about them, she was told that they had "lost their lip plug." The lip plug holds the lower lip open and allows the winds of life to flow freely. The loss of the lip plug meant death.

Rhpis'unt and her bear husband moved away from the others. The winter winds came and the others were moving into caves. Rhpis'unt knew that she was pregnant. She was disgusted with this thought and was glad when her bear husband suggested that they move away from the others. He took her to a cave high on a dangerous cliff.

Her people in the village of Nikae missed Rhpis'unt. The father had sent out warriors to find her, but they returned with no news. Many had looked, searched, and prayed for her. Many gave up looking when they found the bear tracks around her broken basket, but not her brother. He knew that bears did not eat human beings. He knew that she was not dead.

Her brother and his dog Maesk searched for her. They traveled to places no one knew. Soon they arrived at the foot of a dangerous cliff. The dog started to howl. The brother knew that his sister was near and that he would have to climb the cliff. He went back to the village to get help.

Rhpis'unt's bear-man saw the brother and watched him studying the cliff wall. The bear-man knew that if Rhpis'unt's brother got to the cave, there would be trouble. He said to Rhpis'unt, "When your brother comes into the cave, he will kill me. Do not let him tear my skin. Do not let them spoil my meat. Take my bones and burn them; then I can return in spirit and help our children. As soon as I am dead, they will turn into people like you."

Rhpis'unt gave birth that night to twin cubs. They suckled her breasts, tearing her nipples. They grunted loud noises and tore at her with their sharp claws. She cried out in pain as she held and nursed them.

Rhpis'unt's brother arrived with his dog. The others from the village thought him foolish to climb the dangerous cliff. He did, climbing it slowly. Then he threw a burning bush into the cave, smoked out the bear-man, and shot him. Rhpis'unt appeared, coughing and carrying two little cubs. She looked down and saw the bear-man fall against the hard rock at the base of the cliff.

Her brother helped her and the twin cubs down the cliff. They walked to the village. She entered her father's home, and the two cubs took off their bearskins and became human babies. Rhpis'unt taught the people the songs of the Bear-People. She told them to be respectful of the bears for they were relatives. Rhpis'unt grew old and died.

When she was gone, her twins put on their bearskins and walked into the forest. They joined the Bear-People and taught them the ways of human beings.

3. Bear Songs

There was a family that belonged to the Cherokee clan called the Ani'-Tsa'guhi. They had a son who would leave home for days. The father and mother were very worried about this one. He rarely ate at home, and as he grew older, he was gone more and more. His father talked to him of his duties at home. His mother pleaded with him to stay and know his family. The son continued to go at dawn and come home well after dark. The father got angry. He shouted at his son and threatened him, but the son still did not obey.

One morning, the father and mother got up early to watch their son leave on his daily journey. They noticed that he was covered with brown hair. The father confronted his son. "Why is it that you insist on leaving your home every day?" he asked. "Where are you going?"

The son looked down and spoke. "I find plenty to eat in the forest. I have peace. It is beautiful there. It is quiet."

His parents told him that they would leave him alone. He could stay home and they would keep quiet and peaceful.

"No," the boy said, "I must go into the woods and stay there all the time. I am beginning to be different already. I cannot live here anymore. If you wish to come with me, you are welcome. There is plenty to eat, and you will never have to work for it. If you come, you must fast for seven days."

The mother and father thought on this. They were one with their son. They spoke with the elders of the clan in a council. "Here we work hard and rarely have enough food. He says there is always plenty of food without work. We will go with him." All the people of the clan agreed.

All the people fasted for seven days. Then, on the seventh morning, all the Ani'-Tsa'guhi people left their settlement and started for the woods. The son led the way.

The people from the other villages heard of this. They spoke with their elders, who hurried to the people of the Ani'-Tsa'guhi and begged them to stay. But the Ani'-Tsa'guhi were already on their way; they had already taken their path. As the elders spoke with them, they noticed that the Ani'-Tsa'guhi were growing hair all over their bodies, changing before their eyes. The elders asked them what they would eat.

"There is plenty in the woods. We are going where there is always plenty to eat. We shall be called the *yanu* [bears] forever. If you should be hungry, come into the woods, kill us, and eat our flesh. You need not be afraid, for we shall live always." The Ani'-Tsa'guhi taught the other people the song with which to call them. The people were sad and looked down. When they looked up again, they saw a drove of bears going into the forest.

The people who hunt bears were told by the Ani'-Tsa'guhi how to prepare the meat of the bear when they skinned it. They were told to take the hide of the bear and the bones and place them under a pile of leaves. The people could take the meat, but they must leave the hide and the bones buried. The people did this, and when they turned to say a final prayer, they saw a bear rise up out of the leaves and go back into the forest. They then knew that this was great magic, for they had the meat of the bear and the bear had regained his life to live again. The people who hunt remembered to sing the songs.

These are the songs the Cherokee sing to call the bears:

He-e! Ani'-Tsa'guhi, Ani'-Tsa'guhi, akwandu'li e'lanti'
*   ginun'ti;*
He-e! Ani'-Tsa'guhi, Ani'-Tsa'guhi, akwandu'li e'lanti'
*   ginun'ti, YU'!*

In English the words are:

He-e! The Ani'-Tsa'guhi, the Ani'-Tsa'guhi, I want to lay
*   them low on the ground;*
He-e! The Ani'-Tsa'guhi, the Ani'-Tsa'guhi, I want to lay
*   them low on the ground, YU!*

The bear hunter starts out each morning fasting and does not eat until near evening. He sings this song as he leaves the camp. He sings it again the next morning, but never twice on the same day. The second bear song is also sung by the bear hunter in order to get the bear's attention. He sings this on his way from the camp to the place where he expects to find the bear:

He-e! Hayuya'haniwa' hayuya'hanuwa' hayuya hanuwa hayuya'hanuwa Tsituyi nehandu'yanu Tsituyi' nehandu'yanu Yoho-o!

He-e! Hayuya'haniwa' hayuya'hanuwa' hayuya hanuwa hayuya'hanuwa

Kuwahi'nehandu'yanu' Kuwahi' nehandu'yanu Yoho-o!

He-e! Hayuya'haniwa' hayuya'hanuwa' hayuya hanuwa hayuya'hanuwa

Uyahye' nehandu'yanu Uyahye' nehandu'yanu Yoho-o!

He-e! Hayuya'haniwa' hayuya'hanuwa' hayuya hanuwa hayuya'hanuwa

Gategwa'nehandu'yanu Gategwa' nehandu'yanu Yoho-o!

[Recite] *Ule'-nu' asehi' tadeya'stataku'hi' gun'nage astu' tsiki'.*

In English the songs go:

He! Hayuya'haniwa' [four times];
In Tsitu'yi you were conceived [two times] *Yoho!*
He! Hayuya'haniwa' [four times];
In Kuwa'hi you were conceived [two times] *Yoho!*
He! Hayuya'haniwa [four times];
In Uya'hye you were conceived [two times] *Yoho!*
He! Hayuya'haniwa [four times];
In Gate'gwa you were conceived [two times] *Yoho!*

4. Beast Bear-Man

Two Guiana Indian brothers set out in their boat to shoot fish. They told their old father where they were going in case he might have need of them. The younger brother sat at the back steering and singing. The other brother said, "Don't do that. If you make so much noise we shall have no fish and our old father will go hungry."

The younger brother wouldn't stop singing, and his brother was getting angry. "This will not do," he said, "for you are making too much noise. I am going to leave you on the shore to sing." He turned the boat and left his younger brother singing on the shore. That boy kept right on singing. He raised his voice until it was so loud that his older brother could hear him out on the water.

The older brother kept his boat moving until he could not hear the song, and he went on fishing. He shot one fish, then a second, and then a third. Feeling that he had shot enough, he went back to his brother and found him singing louder than ever.

The noise was deafening. It was rolling and roaring high above a sound that he had ever heard his brother sing before. The older brother went home without him, and the old father asked where the boy was. The older brother answered that his brother was screaming so loud that he worried something was wrong with him. The old father did not believe this, so his son told him where the boy was. He could go and hear for himself.

The two went to the spot where the younger brother had last been seen. But no one was there. Then the old father heard an awful noise in the distance, and he followed some tracks to the waterside. They were very deep, and the leaves on each side were crushed, showing that something heavy must have been dragged through that way.

The old father called, "Come, come!" His only reply was a terrible roar, and it frightened him.

Suddenly, the younger son came running after the father. The boy had been changed into an evil *Hebu* beast, which resembled a bear and ate anything. The old father ran to the waterside. He told his oldest son about what he had seen, saying that the boy was on the road behind them and that they must be prepared to shoot as soon as the *Hebu* beast appeared.

Sure enough, the beast came out into the clearing, and they shot him many times. It was a good thing that they did, for the younger son had already changed into a beast from the neck down. He had two big teeth on his belly. If the boy had kept quiet and not sung in the boat, this never would have happened.

5. Bearskin-Woman

The Blackfeet tell of their constellation known as the Great Bear. It was not always up in the sky, for at one time the Great Bear walked the earth.

It all started with a family of nine children. There were seven boys and two girls who helped each other and were very loyal. The father was a kindly man who wanted each one of his children to learn the ways of the Blackfeet and to appreciate the values of the life around them.

On one occasion, the father sent the six older brothers out on a warpath. They were to bring back horses and food. At the same time, he sent his older daughter, Bearskin-Woman, into the forest to gather berries for face paint, dyes, and food. Bearskin-Woman disappeared and did not come back.

The father went out in search of his daughter, taking with him his neighbors and other men skilled at hunting. They searched the forest for Bearskin-Woman but did not find her. The father was worried, for there were grizzly bears in the forest that had been known to enchant young women.

Bearskin-Woman had already been enchanted. Perhaps she had willingly let the spell of a fine grizzly bear overcome her. She had met a fine, strong bear-man in the forest. He was tender, kind, and generous in spirit, and he spoke with her. The two of them found their bonding was strong and chose to unite. The grizzly bear took Bearskin-Woman to his cave. He had food for her, he had a warm place for her to sleep, and he gave himself to her. She was pleased.

The next morning, the father found the tracks of these two. The neighbors helped him and surrounded the grizzly bear's cave. Then the father called out the bear, shooting and killing him. Bearskin-Woman hid in the back of the cave. Her union with the grizzly bear was stronger than her loyalty to her father and family. She hid and waited until everyone had gone home.

She searched for the grizzly bear's body but found that the men had cut it up and taken the meat. The fur of the bear also was gone, and all she found was a small piece of fat with some fur that had been thrown away in the bush. She washed this piece of fur until it was clean and smooth, then put it under the shoulder cloth of her dress. She prayed and called to the spirits to help her understand this feeling that she held within her.

That dark night, she changed into a grizzly bear. Her face grew round. Her hands grew in strength and developed claws. Her back arched and her arms grew in massive muscle. Her legs spread and her anger grew. She reared up on her hind legs and charged into the village. She rushed through the homes, killing everyone, even her own father and mother. She did not kill her youngest brother, Okinai, or her younger sister, Sinopa.

Bearskin-Woman then rushed out of the village, all covered with blood. She fled in the dark to the forest and there regained her original shape.

In the morning, she bathed in the river, then returned to the village and asked what had happened. The people were surprised to see her, but in their grief they did not ask where she had been. Bearskin-Woman ran to her home and took Okinai and Sinopa into her arms. She promised that she would care for them and that they would never want for anything as long as she was there.

Later, Sinopa went to the river to gather water. As she started back home, she came upon her six brothers who were returning from the war path. She told them what had happened, and they listened carefully to her words. They asked Sinopa where their sister had been during the attack on the village. Sinopa told them that she did not know, though she had noticed that her sister kept a piece of bearskin under the shoulder cloth of her dress. The six brothers discussed this and came up with a plan.

They gathered up all the prickly pear cactus they could find, giving it to their little sister to place in front of the home outside the door. She was to go first and tell Bearskin-Woman that her brothers were returning. Sinopa was not to say anything more.

Sinopa hurried home. Bearskin-Woman was busy there, and Sinopa placed the prickly pear cactus all around the house, most of it in front of the doorway. She carefully jumped over the cactus and called out, "Bearskin-Woman, our brothers are returning! They are safe. They are coming up the path."

Bearskin-Woman rushed out of the home to meet them. She stepped on the prickly pear cactus and roared out in pain and anger. In her pain, she changed shape into that of the grizzly bear. The six brothers shot at her as she rushed upon them. They felt the anger, and their arrows missed their marks. Then Okinai ran out from behind his big brothers and shot an arrow of his own into the air. As it flew, the brothers and Sinopa were pushed apart from the grizzly bear.

Okinai shot another arrow, and the bear was pushed out of the village. The arrow never landed; it only succeeded in pushing the grizzly bear farther and farther and farther and farther away from the village and the family.

Then the grizzly bear rushed at them again, and an arrow flew over her head. Okinai waved a magic feather that his father had given him. Bushes and underbrush rose between them and the bear, and Bearskin-Woman stood up on her hind feet and charged the family over the bush. Okinai waved the magic feather again. A lake appeared before Bearskin-Woman.

She swam through the lake and rushed again at the family, raising her ferocious claws over one of the brothers. Okinai waved the feather, and a great tree grew between them and Bearskin-Woman. The family climbed the tree.

As the last four brothers shinnied up the tree, Bearskin-Woman grabbed them by their legs and dragged them to the ground. Okinai shot an arrow into the air. Straight up it flew, carrying his little sister, Sinopa, into the sky. Six more times he shot his arrows straight up into the sky, and each time one of his brothers flew with it, out of sight. The last arrow shot Okinai himself up into the the sky, to be placed next to his family.

The children became stars, and they have the same position in the sky that they had climbing up the great tree. There is a small star at one side, which is Sinopa, and the four huddled at the bottom are the brothers who had been dragged down by Bearskin-Woman. This group of stars is called the Great Bear in the sky.

6. Bear-Man

The Pawnee have a tribe which imitates the way of the bears. This came about through the wisdom of a man who had a beautiful woman.

The man had gone on the warpath, moving with the others. But one day as they traveled, he heard a strange sound. Being familiar with the ways of animals, he followed the sound and found a tiny bear cub that was hungry and helpless.

The man picked up the cub and tied some Indian tobacco around its neck. He held and rubbed the bear until it quieted down. Then he spoke to the bear cub. "You are important, and the Great Spirits will take care of you. I put the tobacco around your neck as a prayer to the spirit Tirawa, who I pray will care for you. I pray that animals will take care of my son when he is born and help him become a wise man." Then the man put the cub down in a safe place with some food and left him again with a prayer.

When this man returned home, he told his woman of the bear cub. He told her how hard it was to leave such a small animal alone in the forest, but to bring it back would have been instant death for the cub. The woman listened to her man's story. She did not know that deep within her womb she was carrying his son. If a woman thinks or ponders about an animal while she is carrying a child, the baby will resemble that animal.

When the man first greeted his infant son, he knew immediately what had happened, for his child looked like a bear cub. The boy grew strong, often running into the forest by himself and praying to the bears.

When the boy was a grown man, he accompanied a war party of the Pawnees as their chief. He had grown into a strong, wise warrior and was appreciated by his people. On this day, the warriors rode into a trap. They were taken completely off their guard by the Sioux.

All forty of the men were killed and their bodies were strewn in the ravines and bushes. This land also was a place of the bears. They watched cautiously from the trees, and once the Sioux were gone came out to review the bodies. A she-bear ran to the Pawnee chief. She called the other bears to her. "This man is the one who brought us smokes, sang songs to us, and gave us food. We must do something to help him, to bring him back."

The bears sat huddled thinking of what they could do. They did not know of a way to return life to someone who had lost it. Night came upon the circle of bears that surrounded the Pawnee chief. Finally, they decided that at first light they would gather all their magic together and chant. The sun would help in the healing.

Sun rose the next day, but clouds tried to block the power from the bears. They worked anyway. Two bears collected all the remains of the Pawnee chief, whom they now called Bear-Man. They put his body together as it should be. They worked their magic over him, and his body slowly grew together. The two bears chanted and made offerings to the sun. They sprinkled corn pollen with their songs. Later that day, Bear-Man began to breathe.

Slowly Bear-Man regained his senses. He moved his arms carefully, stretched his legs in wonder, and turned his head and could see. He sat up and asked the two bears what had happened. They told him how they had brought him to life. Bear-Man looked about as they spoke and saw the bodies of his warriors strewn across the land. He was filled with grief. The bears carried him to their den. They fed him, bathed him, and cared for him. Bear-Man had no hair on his head, for the Sioux had taken his scalp with them. He slowly healed.

The bears taught Bear-Man their magic. They taught him their songs. They showed him their ways and helped him learn the prayers of the bears. They taught him their wisdom. They told him that Tirawa, the great spirit who had made bears, would watch out for him and that he should now return to his people.

Bear-Man walked to the edge of the bear place. "I shall always remember you," he said. "I shall pray for you, and I shall bring you food. If I should die, may it be by growing old, and may you grow old along with me." Then he leaned against a cedar tree. His hands felt the rough bark and a vision came to him. "If you ever are in need," he heard, "take this tree and put it on the fire. Tirawa will know that you are in need and will help you."

The leader of the bears came to Bear-Man. He handed him a bearskin cap, saying, "This is to hide your hairless scalp and keep you strong."

Bear-Man took the cap and returned to his people. He was greeted with amazement, for everyone thought him dead. His father received him joyfully and congratulated him on his return. Bear-Man told his father of the bears. His father smiled, for he knew that his prayer to the little bear cub was answered.

Bear-Man and his father took presents of tobacco, sweet clay, and buffalo meat to the bears. They chanted and prayed to the bears. The bear who had given Bear-Man the cap came out to him one day, hugged him, and said, "Since you have been thoughtful of the bear, I give you my gift. You shall be great, you shall be fearless, and you shall be wise."

Bear-Man became the greatest warrior of his tribe. He started the Bear Dance, lived to be very old, and was respected by all his people.

7. Ma'nabush and the Bear

Ma'nabush left his home and moved in with his uncles, who also were of the Menomini Indian tribe. Ma'nabush helped his uncles and their three sons with the hunting. They would rise early in the morning and go into the woods.

One day, they decided that food was scarce and that they all must go together in order to hunt enough for the winter. They followed a good trail for some time until they came to a place where the path branched. The brothers separated. One of them took the left trail, and the other two went to the right. Each of the brothers had a dog and snowshoes for moving fast through the thick snow.

The older brother was one of the two who had taken the right trail. He had not gone far when one of the dogs scented a bear, which rushed out of the brush and ran. The dogs barked, chasing the bear, and the brothers followed after. They had not gone far when the oldest brother shot an arrow through the body of the bear and killed it.

The two young men took the bear up on their shoulders and carried it to the fork in the trail. There they met their brother. They all returned to their father's wigwam, bringing the bear and saying, "Here is a bear that we killed. We can now eat."

The father shook his head. "When I was your age," he said, "I could shoot two bears in one day. Now there are not so many. We shall be hungry soon." The two brothers said nothing, but they thought on what their father had said.

The next morning, the sons set out on the trail. They followed the same path as the day before. When they got beyond the fork, their dogs started barking. They found a bear hiding in the brush, and when it started off on the right branch of the trail, the dogs chased it and the two boys followed the dogs. The bear ran quickly, and the boys ran far until the middle son drew his arrow and shot the animal. They gathered up the bear on their shoulders and returned to the fork in the trail. There they met their youngest brother, who also carried a bear on his shoulders.

They took these two bears to their father. He shook his head. "When I was young," he said, "I could shoot three bears in one day. But now we shall go hungry."

The sons said nothing but thought on what their father said. The next morning, they awoke early and took the same trail that they had walked before. When they came to the split, they saw the same brush. The dogs scented bears. They barked, a bear started and ran, and this time the youngest of the three sons ran after the bear and shot it. Another bear was found by the dogs. They barked and chased the animal. The other brothers overtook this bear and shot it. They had not had time to lift the bears onto their shoulders when another came out of a hiding place and ran away. The brothers chased this one and soon killed it, too.

They brought all the bears together and took them home to their father. He said, "When I was a young man, I used to shoot four bears in one day. But now we shall go hungry." The sons said nothing but thought on what their father said. He dressed the meat, and the next day they had a feast. They all ate well.

The bears that had been killed were the followers of the Bear-Chief *Ana'maqki'u*. He lived high up on the long mountain that was in the direction the young men had hunted. Every time a bear died, its shadow returned to the home of the chief and there its wounds were visible to all the other bears.

Bear-Chief became angry at the death of his followers, and he decided to capture and destroy the hunters. He told another one of his followers, "Go to the brush at the fork of the trail, and the moment the sons come to hunt, you must return with all the speed you have to this place. The mountain will open and let you in. The hunters will follow. Then we shall punish them."

The next morning, the sons left camp to go hunting. The father prepared the feast in such a manner that the two oldest sons could go off and hunt, leaving the youngest son to help with the cooking. The snow was soft and the snow shoes sank in the mush. Just as the sons were coming to the fork in the road, the dogs started to bark. The bowstring of the elder brother came unfastened and the bowstring of the younger brother broke.

A bear ran out of the brush and quickly took the right-hand branch of the trail. The dogs and the brothers followed it, traveling until they had gone a great distance. Before them, they saw a large, long mountain stretching to the right and left of the trail that they were running on. The follower of Bear-Chief ran to the mountain and it opened to him. The dogs followed, and one brother followed them into the very middle of the mountain. The other running brother became exhausted and was left behind.

When the oldest brother reached the middle of the wigwam, he realized where he was. He saw bears on every side of him. They were sitting around him as if they were in council. The bear that the brother had been chasing lay panting on the ground beside Bear-Chief. The brother gasped, for he realized that he could not shoot the animal, his bow was broken, and he was surrounded by bears.

Bear-Chief asked, "Why are you trying to kill all my people? Don't you see that there are a number with arrows sticking out of their bodies? What have we done to you that you must kill all of us? I will stop this killing by transforming you into a bear."

The second brother came running to his eldest brother. He cried out, "Don't you see that bear? Shoot it, shoot it!" The second brother tried to stab the bear with the arrow, but it broke.

The first brother grabbed him. "Don't you see where you are? Look around you. See where you are standing!"

The second brother struggled forward, trying desperately to kill the bear. But the older brother stopped him. He looked up and saw the angry bears all around. On one side were the followers of Bear-Chief, while on the other were the followers of the chief's sister. She had compassion, and she begged her brother to let the brothers go and not to kill them. He told her that he would not take their lives. "I will transform them in such a way that they will be half-bear and half-human. Their arms and legs will be like the legs of a bear, while the head and body of each shall remain as they are now."

There were two springs of water in the ground near where the brothers stood. When Bear-Chief came to them, he took water from the moss that grew there and rubbed it over the boys' legs and arms. These body parts immediately became like bears' limbs.

The father of the boys waited a long time for his sons. The feast was ready, but his boys were nowhere in sight. Bear-Chief knew that a search would be made for the young men. The father walked until he reached the fork of the trail. He did not know which direction his sons had taken. After a few moments of searching, he discovered the fresh tracks of the snowshoes and followed them into the brush. The father went forward so fast that he stumbled and fell into a gorge that was the hiding place of a strong male bear. He landed flat in the bear's grasp, and the animal snapped his neck and killed him fast.

When the father did not return to the wigwam, his woman knew that something awful had happened. She decided to follow his trail to help him. She started upon the path that her man had taken and found the tracks of the snowshoes. She saw the brush. She moved forward into two bears, and they grasped her neck and broke it, killing her fast.

When the mother and father did not return, the youngest son was worried. He told his sister that he must go out and find them, that he would go to hunt some game and see if he could find his brothers and his parents. The girl cried and begged him to stay, but the young boy insisted on taking this journey.

He made four arrows. One had the shaft of *osa'skimino'na*, another of *pewo'naskin*, the third of *mo'nipio'nowe*, and the fourth of *okapuowe*. He made a small bow and went out to the large tree near the wigwam. He took down his snowshoes and put them on. The right snowshoe was called *dodo'pa* and the left *kuku'kuu*.

A small bark box kept his little dog, called *Waisau'wita*. He let the dog out, and the two of them set out after his parents and the brothers. They followed the trail and walked a great distance, traveling until they came to an immense tree.

The young boy rested against the tree, but the little dog would not. It ran round and round and round and round, barking at the tree. The boy thought that his parents might have been killed here, and he stepped away from the tree. He took one of his arrows out of the quiver, put it into the bow, and shot it into the root. The tree burst into a blaze of fire, with noise bellowing out like thunder. It was quickly consumed by the fire.

The boy thought on this and decided to continue his journey. He hurried on until he came to a fork in the trail. He stopped for a moment to decide which way he should go, saw the snowshoe tracks to the right, and took the trail in that direction. He came to the place where two bears hid in the brush.

Bear-Chief knew what was happening. He saw that the young boy was looking for his brothers and sent a very small bear to the bushes to wait.

The boy reached the brush, and his little dog ran to the bear. The little bear ran out and away for his home. The dog followed, and the boy followed his dog into the large, long mountain as Bear-Chief's wigwam came into sight. The snow was wet and heavy, and the thong of the boy's right snowshoe became loose and broke. He stopped to repair it, but by the time it was fixed, the little bear and dog were far ahead and he could only hear the barking off in the distance.

The boy ran, telling his snowshoe, "We have to hurry or we shall lose both the bear and the dog." The snowshoe sang the song like the *dodo'pa* and the *kuku'kuu*. One sang, "*te'e'e'e'e', te'e'e'e'e'e'*," and the other hummed out, "*hu'u'u'u'u', hu'u'u'u'u'u'*."

The sister of Bear-Chief saw the little boy coming. She had felt compassion for the older brothers of the boy, and now she smiled, seeing the little brother coming towards Bear-Chief's wigwam. The little boy ran after his dog. The mountain opened to take them in, and they ran until they came to the other side. Then the boy stopped. He heard the barking behind him. He ran back to the other side, searching for his dog.

When he stopped, the sound came from the other direction where he had just been. He started to go that way but soon reached the summit of the long, large mountain. He heard the dog below him. The little boy called out, "Let my dog out. I want him!" There was no response. The little boy again called out, "Ana'maqki'u, let my dog out. I need him! If you do not, I shall destroy your wigwam!"

Bear-Chief did not respond, and the little boy went down the mountain. He drew one of his arrows from the quiver and pointed it toward the base of the large, long mountain. He shot his arrow, setting the mountain afire. It burned, and so did Bear-Chief and his followers. But the chief's sister and her followers were spared because she had tried to prevent her brother from hurting the other two brothers.

When the little boy entered the wigwam of the bears, he found his brothers. They stared at him but were unable to move. They had bears' paws and legs. The little boy tried to pull these off, but they would not change or be removed. Then the sister of Bear-Chief said, "Little boy, take some moss out of the spring and let your brothers smell it. They will be who they were if they do this."

The little boy thanked the sister and went to the spring near his oldest brother. He took the wet moss and held it to his brothers' nostrils. The bearskins fell off and dropped from their arms and legs.

The three brothers left the wigwam. They returned to their sister, who was glad to have them back to protect her and gather food. Ma'nabush himself decided to leave on another journey.

Other Animals

The power of animals is central to many Indian tales. The Cherokee believe that the Creator formed this earth as a great floating island in a sea of water. It was suspended by the four cardinal points, and a cord hung down from the solid-rock sky vault. They say that when the world grows old, is used and tired, the cord will break and the earth will sink down into the sea waters. That makes them careful to keep the earth healthy, young, and respected.

In the beginning, when the Cherokee earth was first floating on the waters, the animals were born above it in *Galun'lati,* beyond the arch of the people's birth. The animals were curious to find out what was below the water, so *Daunni'si* (Beaver's Grandchild) asked the little Water Beetle to go exploring with him. They darted over the surface. They searched for a door. They tried to go under, but they could not. Daunni'si then held his breath and dived down as far as he could go. He grabbed hold of a beautiful arch and pulled it *with him to the surface. The arch that he brought up was the opening for the people's earth, which is where we are now.*

The animals knew that this was the way for the people to come to this place. They also knew that the earth was too wet and barely big enough for the animals, so there was no way that it could hold the people, too. The animals were anxious to find a dry place. They sent out birds in all directions to find somewhere that was comfortable. The birds came back, for there was no place they could safely land. They returned to Galun'lati.

Then they sent out Buzzard. He flew over the land and was gone a long time, returning tired and weak. He said that there was no place that would be safe. The animals sang to Grandfather Buzzard, for he held all their hope.

Grandfather Buzzard pulled his strength into his mighty wings. He flew to the place where the Cherokee now are. He flew hard and fast down to the wet land, beating his wings as the animals sang. He slapped the air with his powerful feathers.

The wet earth dried. The animals sang. Grandfather Buzzard felt their courage fill his muscles, and he let the wind from his powerful wings fill the air. The air warmed and the land grew hard and firm. The animals sang their thanks. Grandfather Buzzard perched on this newly made hard, dry land. It was safe. It was good. It was fine. It was as it should be. The animals then called up the people.

The Cherokee people came to this fine land, singing, "We thank you, thank you, Grandfather Buzzard, animals, birds, reptiles, insects, and your songs of hope."

The power of the animals was never forgotten. The magic of the animal world continues throughout this continent in stories.

1. Porcupine vs. Thunderers

An Iroquoian family tells of the coming of the Thunderers. Hi-nua of The People was a very strong hunter. On one occasion, he went hunting with two other men. The days were spent searching for game, but none was found. Hi-nua listened to the spirits of the night. He was a quiet man. Peace was always in him, and his prayers were strong.

After dark, as the others slept, Hi-nua crawled away from the camp and moved with the foxes in the night. As he cautiously searched for game, he fell off an escarpment. This was not good.

Hi-nua lay in the thick underbrush. His left leg burned with the pain of a hundred fires. His foot turned away from his body. Hi-nua called out with his war cry. The owls fluttered hurriedly in the night. The deer raced away.

In the early morning, his companions awoke to follow the cry of Hi-nua. Their interest was not in saving him, but in finding food for their starving families. They cut down branches from the trees and made a rude litter. They carried him, for it was the rule of the people to return a hurt hunter to his home. They grew tired. They put Hi-nua down and walked away to talk. The place where they talked had a cliff which overlooked a large pit. The hunters studied the pit. Then they threw Hi-nua and his litter off the cliff and continued in their search for game.

Hi-nua lay there unaware of what had happened. Cold water stung his face. The smell of wet leather gagged him. He opened his eyes to see an old, withered man leaning over him. The old man giggled when he saw Hi-nua open his eyes. "You are alive. Your friends are more interested in themselves than in friendship."

The old man scratched at his long, grey braids. Wrinkled fingers dipped a cloth into a sap basket and continued to wipe Hi-nua's face. Hi-nua groaned in his pain, "They have left me here to die!"

The old man walked around Hi-nua. "You shall not die. You are strong. I will bring medicine and mend your leg if you will stay here and hunt for me." Beady brown eyes sparkled at Hi-nua.

Hi-nua agreed. Piles of herbs, bundles of tobacco, feathers tied with cotton, and small bowls of cornmeal all were placed neatly around him. The raspy voice of the old one sang for four days. Smoke from the fire enveloped Hi-nua, and the sweat of his body mingled with the smells of the herbs. Hi-nua felt the willow withes wrap around his leg, heard the cry of the sparrow, and felt the rough, old hands mend his broken bone. Hi-nua recovered.

This happened in the fall. The winter's cold was kept away, for Hi-nua hunted and brought food to the old man. The man told Hi-nua of his fear of clouds, and he patted Hi-nua's leg. "If you kill a heavy animal and need help, come and ask me. If there are no clouds, I will help carry your kill home. We must help each other, for that is the way of survival."

Many times Hi-nua would return, asking for the old man's help. Life went well for the two until one day when Hi-nua came across a large elk. It left deep prints in the mud and moved slowly through the grass. Hi-nua killed the elk, and as he stood to ready it, he saw hunters running towards him. He called out to them, for he thought maybe they had been hunting the elk, too.

The hunters stopped and slowly walked towards him. They wore only robes of white feathers—no loincloths or moccasins—just robes of white feathers. They explained that they were known as the Thunderers. Their voices boomed as they whispered, saying to him that they were spirits who hunted evil. They were in pursuit of an evil spirit and asked for Hi-nua's assistance.

"I do not know any evil spirit. What is it that you seek?" Hi-nua was not sure if he could help in such a noble cause. The third Thunderer told of an old man who lived in a pit.

Hi-nua backed away from them. They told him of an old man who feared thunder clouds. This old man had done an evil deed and there was nothing he could do in this life that would make it right. The Thunderers had searched the earth over, trying to find this old man with long, grey braids. If Hi-nua would help them, they would send him home to his lonely mother. Hi-nua agreed.

He ran to the pit and called out to the old man, "I have killed an elk. It is too big for me to carry back by myself. Will you help me?"

The old man stuck his head out of the pit. "Is it cloudy?" he asked. "Do you see any clouds?"

Hi-nua looked up into the sky. "No, there are no clouds. Can you help me?"

The old man climbed out of the pit. He searched the sky for clouds and said, "You are right. There are no clouds."

The two men walked to the east and found the killed elk. The old man and Hi-nua cut up the meat, wrapped it in the elk hide, and started home. They were walking along when the old man dropped his pole, dashing for the pit. Clouds were moving rapidly across the sky, and suddenly a bolt of lightning downed the old man. He tried to get up, but another bolt hit him.

The old man was transformed into an enormous porcupine that raced through the bushes, with quills shooting out of his back like arrows as he ran. The thunder followed the porcupine and burst upon him. One final bolt of lightning left the creature lifeless.

The Thunderers came down out of the sky, saying, "The evil one is now dead. We shall take you to your mother who is fading in her sadness." They gave him a blanket of clouds like theirs. They showed him how to move the wings on the shoulders of the robe.

Hi-nua floated back to his home. He drew aside the door's blanket covering and entered. His mother stared at him. "Do not be frightened," he told her. "I am not a ghost. I have come home."

Hi-nua learned of the power of the cloud-blanket robe and used it many times to protect his people.

2. White Hawk

The Shawnee had a warrior named Waupee, or White Hawk, who lived in the forest alone. He liked animals and birds. He was tall, strong, and one of the most well-known hunters of his tribe. He liked the forest, for to him it held all the spirit that lived within man.

Waupee traveled through the forest finding new animals. One day, Waupee traveled farther than he had before. There, beyond the forest, he saw a clearing; and when he walked out into it, he found a perfect circle. He studied the circle and noticed that it had been made by footprints. The prints, however, did not leave the circle: there were none coming into the circle and none going out. Waupee thought this strange.

That night, Waupee slept in the forest near the clearing. He heard music in the night. He looked up, and descending from the sky was a basket filled with twelve beautiful sisters. They were the daughters of the Star Chief, and the basket was their way of coming down and going up to the sky. Waupee watched the basket. It touched the ground and the sisters got out and began to dance. They had a round magic ring which one of them hit with a stick, making the sound of a drum. Waupee admired these women.

One especially caught his attention. It was the youngest daughter of the Star Chief. She had a round face that shone in happiness. Her smile, her eyes, her round cheeks reflected the joy she felt in her heart as she danced. Waupee could not watch any longer. He ran out of the forest to the women. They saw him.

The women jumped back into the basket and were lifted out of his reach by the time he got to the circle. Waupee watched them. He felt great remorse for scaring them away. He decided to wait until the next night.

The music woke him as he lay waiting. He looked up and the basket came down to the circle. The women were cautious. Waupee did not move. The women danced and danced, laughing and beating on the ring. Waupee thought of how he could get close to the youngest sister. He changed into an opossum.

He scurried near to the edge of the forest, then turned with his tail towards the sisters and backed to them. The sisters laughed. "Look at the opossum. He has come to show us a new game."

The youngest sister called out, "No, let's get out of here. It is a trick!" The sisters climbed into the basket and disappeared. Waupee returned to his own shape and walked back home.

The next night he returned to his hiding place in the forest. On the way he came across an old stump. He kicked it and out came a handful of mice. Waupee called to them. Then he carried the mice-filled stump to the sisters' dancing circle and turned into a mouse himself.

The sisters descended and saw the stump. "Look," said one, "I don't remember that stump. What is it doing there?" Another went to the stump and started hitting it as the mice ran for their lives. The sisters grabbed sticks and killed all the mice except for one. The youngest sister chased it, and as she was ready to hit the mouse with a stick, it changed into Waupee. He grabbed her and did not let her go. The other sisters jumped into the basket and rose up into the sky, leaving their youngest sister behind.

Waupee took his woman home. He tried to make her happy. He missed that glow of joy that she had on her face when she danced. Now she did not dance at all.

In time, his woman gave birth to a boy. She asked if she could return to her father and show him the son. Waupee felt for his woman, for sadness was constantly in her. He took her to the place of the circle in the clearing, let her get into the basket with his son, and watched as she ascended into the sky.

Waupee went back to the circle every night. His woman did not return. He felt a sadness enter into his spirit. He missed his woman and hurt with the pain of not seeing his son. As time went by, Waupee stopped going to the circle. He stayed home and sang of his son and of his woman.

Waupee's woman played with her sisters up in the sky. She taught the boy of her own father's ways. But when the son grew to resemble Waupee, she remembered her man. She went to her father and asked him if there was a way she could bring Waupee up to live with them. The Star Chief told her that if her man could bring a piece of every animal that lived in the forest with him, he could live in the sky.

Waupee's woman left her son with her sisters and came down in the basket. She went to Waupee and told him of his testing. Waupee spent four days gathering bits and pieces of the mammals, birds, and snakes that lived in the forest. On the night of the fourth day, he went to the circle.

The basket was lowered. He was lifted up to Star Chief's home. There he saw his son. The Star Chief told all the people to pick a part of an animal, bird, or snake from the basket. Some chose a foot, some a wing, some a tail, and some a paw. Those who chose tails or paws were changed into animals or snakes and ran away. The others turned into birds and flew away.

Waupee chose a white hawk's feather. His woman and son did the same. They spread their wings and descended with the other birds to the earth. Their families are still living in the forest today.

3. Seneca Medicine

In the beginning of life, a man went into the woods to find food. He was alone, not by choice, but because there was no one else. He camped out in a flat plain and was awakened in the dark of night by the sound of a beating drum. The man could not sleep with the beating of the drum. It was rude for someone to be beating a drum in the dark of night. He got up and tried to find the thoughtless person.

When he arrived near the place of the drum, he saw a field. On one side of the field was corn, and on the other side was a large vine with four squashes on it. Three ears of corn grew out of the ground, apart from the other corn plants.

He had no idea what this meant. Going back to camp, he lay down on his bedroll, but was startled by the sound of a man's cough. He turned, and there was a man looking at him and shouting, "You found the sacred fire! I am after you! I will kill you! You should die!"

The man jumped up to confront his enemy. People assembled around them—people he did not know. In the middle of everyone, a fire started, and from it grew a laurel bush. The people began to dance around it. They were singing and rattling gourd shells. He asked them to tell him what they were doing.

One of the people heated a stick over the burning laurel bush. Suddenly he thrust it through the man's cheek. He fell to his knees in pain. Another person took some corn from the corn plant and rubbed it on the wound. The pain was gone. Another took a hot stick and thrust it through the man's leg. He screamed out in agony. The people took some squash and rubbed it on his leg. It healed. All the time they sang, chanted, and beat the drum. The people told him this was the medicine song. They taught it to him.

He left in the morning and returned home, carrying some of the plants with him. He sat on the floor of his home and thought of this magic. He was alone. There were no more people in his village, for they had left long ago. He knew he should share this magic, but with whom?

That night, he returned to the area where the ceremony had taken place. He heard the beating of the drums. He saw the people gather to dance in a circle. Then, as he watched, the people turned into bears, beavers, and foxes. He stood to leave, but when they heard him the animals ran off into the night.

This man wandered until he found the Seneca people, and it is said that his coming was the origin of their great medicine. The people still sing when they make the medicine, every time the deer changes his coat. They burn tobacco in times of fear. The medicine still works.

4. Devilfish Promise

Gitlin was a young Haida warrior. His wife and two children went with him every day when he fished. They took spears, sharp hooks, and the boat. They landed their boat on a small island where the waves were still and the fish plentiful.

Gitlin and his wife speared devilfish, which do not have much meat even though they are the largest of the rays and resemble the octopus. The speared devilfish were dropped into an open basket on the shore, then were cut up and used for bait to catch the larger fish.

Gitlin noticed his children wandering up into the brush of the island. He called to his wife, "I want to see what is on the other side of the island and look into the brush. I shall be back before midday. Keep the children here with you in case there is danger."

Gitlin swung his spear as he walked through the brush. Birds, small snakes, and frogs moved out of his way. He climbed to the top of the mountain. It was rocky and there were caves that had been formed by the wind and water. He walked to the shore and entered a large opening. Chunks of seaweed, starfish, and mussel shells lay all about the floor. In the back of the cave there was something glowing.

He waded into the water above his knees. He could see something glimmering underwater and he wanted to find it. He continued to wade in deeper and deeper. Something long tangled around his right leg. Gitlin reached down to free himself, when something grabbed his hand. A tentacle whipped around his waist and pulled him down under the black waters of the cave and out of sight.

Gitlin's woman waited. She walked through the brush, holding the children. They called and called. They climbed the mountain where the rocks were and called and called. There was no answer. They walked along the shore, looking, calling, and still they did not find him. The sun was setting and darkness would soon make it impossible for them to return home.

Gitlin's woman put the children into the boat. She sang a song of hope as she rowed on the water. She told the Haida people of her husband's disappearance. She said a prayer as she lay down to sleep.

Gitlin awoke, gasping for air. He was in the bottom of the sea. He held his throat, trying to breath.

"You do not need to worry. You can breath as we do now. Try it." A maiden with long, black hair smiled as she swam over to him.

Gitlin shuddered. Her body was only bones. "Who are you—what are you?" he asked, pushing away from her. "I am the proud daughter of the Devilfish Chief. I am called Hanax." She put her bony fingers around his arm.

"Please don't touch me. I would like to go home. I meant you no harm." Gitlin studied her face.

"Oh, no, I have waited a long time for a mate to arrive. My father brought you here. You are to be my man. You are to be the father of our children." Her eyes glowed.

Gitlin thought of his woman and his children. He wondered if they would follow him into the cave.

"Come, my father the Devilfish Chief is waiting for us. Come!"

She pulled Gitlin through the blue-green water. She took him to a deep cavern that was surrounded with seaweed. Huge shells decorated the cave. There, sitting on a cushion of soft seaweed, was the Devilfish Chief. He was a huge, black octopus with green-yellow eyes. "Welcome to our world," he said. "We have been waiting for you. You are to marry my daughter Hanax. You will become the Prince of the Sea when you and my daughter are one."

Gitlin stepped forward. "Great Chief, I do not understand your world. I could not live here for long. I need air, sun, and the freshness of the winds to keep my spirit alive. I feel that your daughter deserves someone who can appreciate your world better than I."

The Devilfish squinted at Gitlin. "Are you saying that you won't marry my daughter?"

Gitlin shook his head. "No, I need to go back to my own world."

Hanax went to her father's side. "Let him go back for a while. He could go back and say good-bye to his family and then return here."

The Devilfish Chief studied Gitlin. "All right, you may return for four days. Then you go to the cave on the island. We will wait for you there."

Hanax brought two canoes. She sat in one and Gitlin got into the other. The canoes moved through the water without anyone paddling. They ascended to the surface, lifted into the air, and floated over the water to the Haida village. Hanax waved to Gitlin as her canoe descended under the waves.

Gitlin returned to his home. There he hugged his wife and children. He could not tell what had happened, for he did not want them to worry. Each morning when he went to his boat to fish, there were presents from Hanax. His woman questioned him about them, but he just laughed and tossed them back into the sea.

Gitlin was very happy and stayed close to his island. Sometimes he thought about Hanax and the Devilfish Chief, but he decided that he was safe and that there was no need to worry.

One evening, there was a feast on the shore. The Haida people were inside the great wooden house singing, dancing, and eating. The door was blocked with a large wooden beam to keep out anyone who might want to cause harm while the people were celebrating. Nonetheless it opened. The door opened and air from outside bent the fires. The people froze and stared.

A large, black shadow came through the door. It floated over the ground. It came to Gitlin and stared down on him.

Gitlin's body screamed out in pain. His arms shrank into his body. His legs became boneless. He grew four tentacles. His head shrank and became one with his body. His eyes became huge and fearful.

The large, black Devilfish Chief's long tentacle shoved Gitlin's devilfish body toward the door. The people moved out of the way. They followed the figures to the shore. There they saw a beautiful maiden. The maiden's body shrank, grew long tentacles, and became a devilfish as well. She put her tentacle around the other devilfish, Gitlin. They got into two canoes, which both hovered over the water, then descended under the waves. No one ever saw them again.

5. First People

Eskimo Wolverine wandered along the river bank. He saw Muskrat swimming at the edge of the water and called out, "Who are you? Are you a man or a woman?"

Muskrat answered, "I am a woman," and Wolverine told her that she could be *his* woman. "I cannot be your woman," she said. "I live in the water and you live on the land!"

Wolverine smiled. "You can live on the land as well as in water." With that, Muskrat went up on the bank to Wolverine and told him where she wanted her home. They ate their suppers, and in the morning they built a house.

Soon after this a child was conceived. Wolverine told Muskrat that this would be White Man, father of all the white people. This child was born from its mother's vulva.

In time, a second child was to be born. Wolverine said that this would be Indian, father of all Indian people. This child was born from its mother's mouth.

Then a third child was to be born. Wolverine announced that this child would be Eskimo, father of all Eskimo. It was born from all of the being of Muskrat Mother.

A little late, a fourth child was conceived. This was to be Iroquois, and it was born from the mother's nose. When the fifth child was born, Wolverine declared that it would be Black, father of all black people. This child was born from its mother's ear.

These children remained with their parents until they grew to be adults, having been taught the ways of the animals. One day, their mother called them together and announced that it was time to separate. She sent each one to a different place on the land. She directed them to go to the animals whenever they were in need of anything. The animals, she said, would have everything—and they would always share with her children.

6. Gopher's Wisdom

The Sioux tell of a younger brother who lived with his older brother and that man's two wives. The younger brother went hunting and came back with an owl he had shot. As he walked towards the older brother's teepee, one of the wives came out to meet him. She asked her brother-in-law for the owl, but he refused to give it to her. She cried and cried and cried. He would not give it to her. The woman took a sharp rock and cut up her face. She scratched her cheeks, her hands, her thighs, and she cried and cried. When the older brother came home, she told him that his younger brother had done this to her. That made him angry, so he called a friend to come and take the younger brother out to an island and leave him there. When the friend returned, he was allowed to marry this abused wife.

The friend could not stand to live with this abusive woman and he turned himself into Gopher and left the village.

The younger brother lived alone on the island. He ate all the edible berries. He tried to catch fish, but they would not get near his traps. He became very hungry and very sad. One day, as he lay sleeping, he heard a noise near him. He looked down and saw three wild turnips pushing up from the ground. He ate these for several days, then was hungry again.

He slept, and while asleep he heard a noise. There at his feet was a small animal. It was Gopher.

He caught Gopher, painted him for identification, and prayed to him for help in getting off the island. Then he released the animal, and Gopher plunged into the lake, disappearing under the surface. After a time there was a movement in the water.

A tremendous monster rose out of the lake. It was huge with very large horns. The monster spoke to the brother, telling him to climb onto his back and take hold of his horns. "I shall carry you to shore, but you must tell me if you see a cloud." The younger brother agreed and they started across the lake. Then the brother saw a large cloud moving towards them but didn't want to say anything to the monster until he was on the shore. He waited to be let off, and when he was ready to tell about the cloud, lightning shot out of it and killed the monster.

The younger brother ran. He heard crying as he approached some trees. "Oh, Oh, Oh, Oh, our grandfather is dead. Our grandfather has been killed, Oh, OH, OH!"

The younger brother carefully approached the sound of the crying. He searched for those who were making this horrible sound. There on the ground he saw buffalo skulls— and they were the ones who were crying. He took out his knife and killed them. Then he walked on his journey until he came to a lodge. An old woman lived there, and she called out to him, "Oh, my lost son, come home to me!" The brother walked over to her. She said that she had been cooking meat for him. The brother was very tired, and very careful of this old woman. He followed her inside and she gave him some meat to eat. He ate it and felt even more tired. Lying down, he pretended to go to sleep.

He cautiously watched this old woman. He saw her painting her legs and noticed that they were growing! While she was busy doing this, the brother sprang upon her and stabbed her with a crane's bill. The old woman screamed a painful, horrible scream, and the terrified brother ran out of the lodge. Later, he looked back inside to see what had become of the old woman. He saw that her body lay across the fire. He pushed it onto the logs, added more wood, and in this way he burned her and the whole lodge. If he had not done this, women would have the power to increase in size and kill men.

After this, he went on his way and came to another lodge where a woman invited him to come in and have food. He watched her cooking, and as she bent over to stir the food in the pot, he noticed that she had a hole in the top of her head. He could see that she would slyly take some of her brains out and put them into the pot. The younger brother watched with amazement. He knew this was a trick, and he leaned back and called Gopher to him. Gopher dug up next to his leg, and the younger brother told him, "If this food is evil, gnaw a hole in the bottom of the pot and let the evil food drain out. If the food is good, then I shall eat it."

Gopher went under the cooking pot and gnawed a hole in it. The evil food disappeared out the bottom. The younger brother pretended to be eating the food as the woman watched him. She had mixed poisons in the food and was waiting for him to become unconscious and die. The brother yawned and lay back to sleep. The woman did the same. The brother watched the fire. There were stones in it that were red hot, and he pulled them out with a stick and quickly dropped them into the hole in the woman's head. She jumped up, screaming in pain, and fell into the fire. The younger brother let her burn there. If he had not done this, women would still mix the poison of their brains in the food that they feed to men.

The younger brother went on his way. He came to another lodge. An old woman was waiting for him. She said, "Come here, my son. I have been waiting for you."

A voice from inside said, "Son? A man? Is there a man out there?"

The old woman said, "Yes."

The other voice responded, "I think I have seen one of those before."

The younger brother went inside. There were two women, sisters, and they fought over him. Each one wanted him to sleep with her. The younger brother solved the argument by taking the younger woman's bed. He lay there. He was very tired. After a while he heard the sound of the teeth in her vagina grating together. He knew of this. He took the crane's bill and shoved it up her vagina until he had killed her quietly.

He went into the other sister's bed and lay quietly with her. Soon he heard the teeth in her vagina grating. He took the crane's bill and shoved it up her until she was dead. If he had not done this, all women would be dangerous lovers.

The younger brother continued on his way. Soon, he came to a cloud that stood out on the top of the hill. As he came to it, he turned to see animals following him. There were all kinds of animals, with a woman walking in the middle of them. He took off his clothes and stood naked. He took mud and rubbed it on his body. He picked up a long, withered branch and bent over it like an old man.

The woman came up to him. She told the animals, "Don't hurt this one, for he is old and wise. Leave him and we shall move on to another." The animals followed her. The last of them were small, and the brother killed and ate two birds, for he was very hungry. This is the way that people came to eat birds.

The younger brother walked on to another lodge. He saw a poor woman going out for water. When he spoke to her, he realized that she was his sister. She was worn and bent. She told him that her husband had beat her and ordered her to do all the heavy work. The younger brother hid in their lodge. When his sister's husband came home, he waited. When the man started to beat on his wife, the brother came out and killed him. That is why cruel husbands now are punished by their wives' families.

The younger brother moved on his way. He came to a camp of people. His brothers were there and his father. The father was very old, and when he saw this son he had thought dead, the overjoyed man collapsed. The younger brother announced that he had been out learning from the ways of life. The others laughed at him and said that they would not feed him. He would have to find his own food.

The younger brother hunted and killed many buffalo, leaving them in a big pile and going back to tell his people. They ran to the pile, but there were a great many birds and cats already eating the meat. The people fell upon them, fighting for the buffalo, but the birds and cats killed their attackers. This is why animals now eat the flesh of men.

7. Wolf Clan Lesson

The Nass River people of the Northwest coast tell of a time when the people caught more salmon than they could use—so many that excess fish were thrown away, carelessly. There was a canyon near the head of a fast-moving river where the people could always find food, salmon, berries, and skins. The villagers who lived near there were wealthy traders. They were respected on account of their wealth.

Over time, this wealth made the younger people lazy, thoughtless, and cruel. They would kill small animals and leave the meat to rot for the crows. The Officers called the young people to a meeting. Some young people came, but others did not. The Officers told the young people that the Chief of the Sky would show his anger at their thoughtlessness. The young people listened, went out, and did as they pleased.

One young man experimented with the salmon. He found that if a fish were slit down the back, it could still swim. He put burning pitch in the slit salmon and placed it back into the water. The salmon frantically swam in circles, lighting up the river. The men of the Wolf Clan thought this amusing.

The Wolf Clan caught fish for this purpose alone. They lit up the river with burning salmon at night. The pain of this cruel amusement was felt in the sky. Thunder rolled out across the land as the Wolf Clan netted the salmon. The fish cried out in their pain, and the cruelty of this slow death was echoed to the Great Above.

The Officers called the Wolf Clan to a meeting, but the men only laughed. They didn't go to the meeting, for they were eager to light up the river. They lit the hot pitch that lay in the slits of the struggling salmon. They pushed the fish into the river and sat back to watch. The sky grew dark. Thunder shook the land. The earth rattled. Rocks fell down from the canyon into the river, crushing the suffering salmon and bringing them a quick, painless death.

The Wolf Clan laughed. "It is the ghosts waking up," someone said. "They want to see the river light up with the floating fish." The Wolf Clan men returned the next night to repeat their cruelty. The night sky rolled out in anger, and the sound of drums reverberated across it. The Wolf Clan men became afraid.

The sound grew louder and louder and louder and LOUDER. The noise became deafening as the mountain broke open. Black pitch from every salmon that was ignited poured forth and surrounded the people.

They tried to escape, but burning, red-hot pitch blocked the rivers. Fire poured down through the forest, fell from the sky, and enveloped the people. A few got away or we would not know of this story.

It is said that the young men of the Wolf Clan carried the burning, red-hot pitch on their backs and turned into burning salmon that suffer in the bottom of the Nass River. They lie frozen in the black pitch of the mountain forever.

8. Buffalo-Maiden

There was once a village, near the Arikara on the prairie, made up of the Buffalo-Ones. The Buffalo-Ones in those days were not so different from human beings, though they wore horns.

In the Buffalo village, they kept the sacred bundle called "Knot in the Tree." They would sing chants of respect for four days, and after that the Buffalo medicine man would go to an ancient cottonwood tree and strike a knot in its trunk three or four times. Then they would hear people crying and talking under the ground.

After the Buffalo-Ones did this several times, a great many people came out of the tree. Cut-Nose, first man, warned the people of these Buffalo-Ones, who hunted human beings like animals. Cut-Nose ran fast out onto the land, but many of the others who followed him were killed and cut up for a great feast. Cut-Nose hid, and when it was safe he ran back to the tree. He leapt inside and warned the other people. They stopped coming out.

The flesh of the dead people was then cut up and the Buffalo-Ones danced as the meat was put on drying frames.

One young man peered out of the tree. There was no one around to see him. He could hear the sound of the Buffalo-Ones, but he could not see them. He climbed out of the tree and ran to hide among the bushes. There were small animals to eat as well as some berries. He moved constantly from one place to another so that he would not be found.

One day, he saw a beautiful woman. She was dressed in white leather. Her hair hung below her knees and she moved with grace. He noticed that she wore horns in her hair. Her beauty captivated him. He followed her. He saw her go into a fine painted tipi. He followed her. She asked him into her tipi. She asked him to sleep with her. They lay wrapped in her robe of white skin. She gave him some meat. He slept. When he awoke there was no tipi.

Buffalo-Woman told him how the Buffalo-Ones wanted to become animals. But he was the only one who could bring about the magic. He would have to be brave and come into great danger, for he would have to meet the Buffalo-Ones who eat flesh. She told him that he would have to go into Buffalo-Chief's tipi.

She covered him in a buffalo skin and led him as far as the guards. Some thought they could smell human meat, but told them that it was only blood that had been left on the ground. The man crawled into Buffalo-Chief's tipi. He moved to a pile of animal skins and lay down to rest. Soon he heard Buffalo-Chief chanting and learned the way to use the ash cane to strike the magic tree when calling the food people. The man did not dare fall asleep for fear of being caught.

In the morning, when Buffalo-Chief went out to lead another great hunt, Buffalo-Woman came to the man. She showed him the place of the people-meat-drying. He climbed the ladder to find human legs, arms, breasts, and some heads. He became filled with rage, and this gave him strength to continue.

Buffalo-Woman took him to a sacred tree. She showed him how to cut staves and trim bows. He took the twigs and canes and made arrows. He used strips of skin to make bow strings, fashioning as many as he could. Then Buffalo-Woman went with him to the tree. She called to Cut-Nose, telling him to take a bow and arrow for shooting a Buffalo-One. Everyone that followed was to do the same.

The next day, they took bows to the sacred tree and hid them underneath a buffalo skin. Buffalo-Chief came with his warriors. He chanted while he struck the tree three times and then four times. There was a sound of human voices. Cut-Nose came running out, grabbed his bow, and ran beyond the Buffalo-Ones. The other people came up, ran over to the place of bows and arrows hiding, grabbed what they needed, and ran. They did this quickly. They shot at the Buffalo-Ones. The Buffalo-Ones returned to the meat-storage house. They took with them pieces of human flesh, which they held under their armpits.

The Buffalo-Ones did not know how to fight. As they were hit with arrows, each turned into a real buffalo. They learned to graze on the prairie grass instead of eating people.

Buffalo-Woman married the man, and their children founded the Arikara nation. Whenever the Arikara use buffalo for food, they leave the lump under the animal's foreleg, for it is human meat of their ancestors.

9. KoKo Wisdom

The Zuni's Rain Priest had a son who was very different from the other boys in the village. The Rain Priest had many brothers; yet, because of an unexpected illness, he never got to share this information with his only son. The Rain Priest's woman was never known, and many wondered if she was a person or a spirit. The Rain Priest died leaving his son an outcast, so the boy decided to live with his grandmother beyond the village.

The grandmother was known for her scary ways. She was a very unattractive woman with a sharp, shrill voice that frightened away docile beings. People stayed away from the grandmother. They stayed away from both the son and the grandmother.

The two lived poorly, and they were mistreated and very hungry. The grandmother was told in a dream of their family living east of the Place of Turkey Tracks. Grandmother knew that she could not walk that far. She told Grandson that if they were to survive they must pursue the dream vision. Grandson left early in the morning to find the Place of Turkey Tracks.

He traveled east, walking across a small stream where he met some little turkeys. These turkeys were the size of your palm. They clucked to Grandson. They pecked on his moccasins, and he followed them to their home. He sat down in the mud turkey shack. His head was hunched down into his shoulders and his hair fell onto his knees as he watched the turkeys busily cluck to each other.

The walls of this short, small home were made of mud decorated with shields, bows and arrows, strings of beads, braided corn of different colors, and very small katsinas. Grandson noticed the intricate work in the katsinas. The small, drawn hands showed the knuckles, fingers, ribs, and knees of the katsina spirit. Each line of the face was carefully placed. They were as perfect as the spirits themselves.

One of the turkeys pecked him on the knee. This immediately brought Grandson's attention to the little turkey. The turkey bent down, gobbled a strange item, then coughed up a bundle of red beads into Grandson's lap. Grandson carefully picked up the fragile string of beads and put it around his neck. The same turkey bent down, gobbled, then choked and coughed up a string of burned turquoise into Grandson's hand.

One by one, each little turkey came to Grandson and coughed a long turkey feather into his hand. The little turkeys stood aside as Grandson gathered the feathers together. A large gobble sound came from the back of the mud home. There, walking toward Grandson, was a taller turkey with colorful feathers. He strutted to Grandson and said, "With these feathers you are to make prayer sticks upon your return home. If you need help, all you have to do is hold up the prayer sticks." The little turkeys taught Grandson songs to sing, prayers to pray, and chants to bring him safety. They told him what to do with the beads when he got to Zuni.

Grandson returned home. He did as he was taught. Grandmother gave him willow withes to hold the feathers, and he made prayer sticks and planted them in the empty, dry cornfield that had belonged to his ancestors. He sang the songs, chanted the chants, and prayed the prayers that he had been taught by the little turkeys.

That night, while the grandson and his grandmother slept, the little turkeys came to Grandson's home. They walked through the door blanket and changed into men. They moved silently through the house, dropping leather pouches, fur robes, blankets, corn, cotton thread, and buckskin clothing. As they walked back out into the early dawn, they turned back into little turkeys. They ran scattering in every direction.

Grandson and Grandmother awoke to find the turkey gifts. Their four-room home had one room filled from floor to ceiling with corn. There were ears of red corn. There were ears of white corn. There were ears of blue corn. There were ears of yellow corn. The corn mysteriously regenerated so that the room was never less empty or more full. It always contained the same amount of corn. They knew not to question this magic.

This wealth of corn made the people more suspicious of them. Everyone still stayed away. Grandson knew Grandmother's loneliness was a burden to her.

Then Grandmother told Grandson of his uncle and suggested it was time for Grandson to visit him. He traveled all day to the west without meeting anyone; however, when he arrived, Uncle was standing outside waiting for him. The older man was very glad that he had come and taught him a song and many dances. Grandson was given turquoise moccasins, high leggings made of buckskin, parrot feathers, and a kilt. His uncle dressed him, showing him the correct way to wear these ceremonial clothes. Grandson learned that his uncle was a *KoKo,* a katsina spirit holder.

Grandson took these items with him to show Grandmother. He told her that the uncle had asked him to clean their home. So Grandmother braided chamisa, sage, rabbitbush, and juniper branches. She watched him clean. The grandson stood up and sang his uncle's song. Grandmother lit the braided bundles of branches and blessed each room of their home with the smoke. Grandson's beads shook and made a strange noise.

Early the next day, Grandson rose and went out to hunt. Unlike his usual return, he came bringing home a deer. Grandmother prayed over it, and Grandson chanted as he cut up the meat and cured the skin.

When spring came, Grandson removed the prayer sticks from the ancestor's field and planted the seeds of yellow corn, blue corn, red corn, and white corn. He planted seeds of watermelon, pumpkin, squash, and different beans. He sang to each seed the song of a man courting a maiden. He prayed to each seed that it might grow as a child. He danced between the rows, spraying water on each mound. In a few days, the plants grew and blossomed. Grandson went out into the field and sang, chanted, and danced, giving thanks. The plants bore food.

Grandson took this food to the village, but people only stared at him. They pulled their children away as he passed. The Ones Who Hold Magic clicked their tongues in disapproval. Grandson spread his blanket and opened his baskets. He placed the ripe ears of corn out; the large, ripe squashes; the thick, colored beans. And he watched.

Men looked over him. Children ran around him. Women shook their heads as they passed him. But one Rain Chief knelt at his blanket. "You have learned much. You have learned to respect the land and it has returned the favor. You have gained in knowledge." The Rain Chief traded with Grandson. The others watched the squash that they had wanted go with the chief. Then people pushed to be first in line to trade. Grandson went home with much more than food that night. He had earned respect.

The people liked Grandson's produce and they spoke kindly to him. He next brought Grandmother to the village. Her face smiled and the harsh wrinkles disappeared. She busied herself with the trade, and her raspy, shrill voice was soft and kind. The other old ones came and traded with her. They finished by trading stories. Grandmother's eyes sparkled.

The Ones Who Hold Magic did not like this at all. They told the people to stay away from the evil grandmother and her ugly grandson. The people did not listen. They knew what they saw. The Ones Who Hold Magic became angry. They no longer had control over the people. They decided to do something about it.

They met together. One Magic Holder said that he would turn into a caterpillar and eat up all of Grandson's plants. Before the sun's rising he was in Grandson's field devouring the corn.

Rain Priest heard the plan and went to Grandson's home to tell him. Grandson unwrapped his bedroll; pulled out his beads and burned turquoise; and followed his uncle's song, chant, and dance. He walked outside and clapped his hands four times. The caterpillar flew through the air to land in Grandson's hand. He begged for his life.

Grandson said, "I will let you live, but you will live down in the bottom of the world. You will always be as you are now, and you will come out only in the middle heat of summer when the weeds have grown. At that time you will live on weeds." He threw the caterpillar deep into the earth.

A few days later, the Ones Who Hold Magic had another meeting. They decided that they would make a grey worm which would eat up everything in the grandson's field. One was picked to do this job. Rain Priest came to Grandson's home again, telling him of the plan. Grandson performed his uncle's ceremony, caught the grey worm, and sent him to the bottom of the world, to come to the surface only to eat weeds in the heat of summer.

A blue worm was sent to the field. The grandson caught him and sent him to the bottom of the world. A red worm was sent to eat the crops, and he also was sent to the bottom of the world. Finally, the leader of the Ones Who Hold Magic said that he would go as a butterfly and lay eggs in the corn, squash, pumpkins, and beans. The eggs would hatch and the crop would be ruined by the caterpillars.

Rain Priest told Grandson, and the boy took the cotton thread, the red beads, the burned turquoise, and a stick to make a butterfly snare. The next day, he took it with him to his field. He saw the butterfly and caught it. Grandson told the butterfly that it would be that shape forever and live in the hot southern lands. The Ones Who Hold Magic now were frightened of the grandson, for they knew that he held magic.

The next day, Grandson went hunting and brought home a fine deer. He and his grandmother were invited to the village feast day and participated in the dances.

10. Faithless Woman

Once there was a man who was not very smart, but he was kind. His name in Iroquois meant "Hemlock Bows." Hemlock Bows would go hunting every day, and he always had good luck, for he said his prayers, gave his thanks, and was respectful to kill only what he needed. He had a woman who bore him a son. She worked hard fixing the game that Hemlock Bows brought home. She bore Hemlock another child, a girl. But then she became tired of all this work. When the girl was three years old, the woman became uninterested in Hemlock Bows.

Hemlock Bows would go out hunting in the morning. His woman would call her son and daughter and send them on a long errand. She would wash her hair, unroll her ceremonial dress, put on her woven belt, and go out looking for other men. The children would return to a cold home, no food, and fear.

One night, Hemlock Bows asked his son to help with the skinning of the meat. Hemlock Bows talked about the ways men hunt, the songs that hunters sing, and the honor among animals and men. His son was very quiet. Hemlock Bows took his son's silence seriously. "What is it that concerns you, my young hunter?"

Big, brown eyes grew wide. "Would you like to go out on a hunt with me tomorrow?" the father asked. The son was quiet.

"You are deeply concerned about something," said Hemlock Bows, confronting him. "Hunters never keep secrets from one another. It is not good for the spirit of unity. Tell me, what is it that troubles you?"

The brown eyes looked down out of respect. "Father, I cannot go with you on a hunt. I cannot leave my sister alone here. She would be frightened and be eaten by large animals."

Hemlock Bows knelt before his son. "Your mother is here to teach her the ways of the women. She will be taught by your mother."

The boy shook his head. "Mother is not here during the day. She meets other men in the forest who give her things. She does not come home until dark, and she makes us tell you things which are not the way they are."

Hemlock Bows reached out to his son. He lifted the boy's head and saw the seriousness in his face. "This is the way it is after I leave in the morning?" The young boy nodded.

"It is good that you told me. This is not right. You have done well to share your concerns with me. Now we must think of how to set this right."

The next morning early, Hemlock Bows left home as he always did; but instead of going hunting, he hid. His woman sent the children on an errand. She dressed and started out with her ax and long strap, used for cutting wood. She passed Hemlock Bows on her way but did not see him hiding.

Hemlock Bows followed her closely. His woman came to a large black-ash tree. She pounded upon the trunk with her ax. She sang a song of courting. A man came out from behind the tree. The man knelt down in front of her and placed something at her feet. She grunted acceptance of the gift. The man took her in his arms. He kissed her, touched her breasts, and was very forward with her. She let the man do these things to her.

Hemlock Bows took his bow and arrow and shot. The arrow missed them and hit the tree. Hemlock Bows's woman took her ax, strutted over to Hemlock Bows and beat him with the ax. He fell down unconscious. She went home, put her son and daughter out in the snow, and set the cabin on fire. The children ran to her side. She threw them down in the snow and yelled at them to leave her alone. She went to the village.

Hemlock Bows came round. He staggered home to find his children shivering in the snow. His home was ashes. He stared in disbelief at the place that had taken him years to build. Everything they had was gone. Their food, their traditional ceremonial fetishes, his bows and arrows, their bedroll. He was astounded at his woman's evil.

"Where is the dog?" Hemlock asked, and the children started searching for it. The dog had run into the forest, and they found it there. Then Hemlock Bows decided that he would find his woman. He left his children with the dog at the home of the ashes. The dog dug a shelter in the snow for the children. They waited for their father to return with food, but Hemlock Bows did not return. It became dark.

Before dawn, the children and the dog started to walk to the village. The brother carried his little sister on his back. She saw a flock of large, white turkeys. She called out that she wanted one right away. Her brother set her down and ran to get a white turkey. While he was chasing the birds, a bear carried off his little sister. The dog followed the bear.

The brother returned to find his sister gone. "The spirits are against me. I have no purpose. My mother has burned our home, my father is gone, my sister has been eaten by a bear, and the dog has left me. I shall go to another place!" He took a leather strap and hung it from a branch. He tied it around his neck as he sat on the branch. He jumped, sure that he would die. The strap broke and the boy landed face down in the snow. He sat up, smiling, and said, "I was meant to stay here."

He went to a lake. He walked in the water, for it was shallow. A great fish swam up behind and swallowed him whole. But the brother sang the song his father had taught him, and it made the great fish weak.

Not far from this place lived a kindly woman with her daughter. They saw the great fish, caught it, and cut it open to find Hemlock Bows's son still alive. He told them all about himself and his family. They asked this young man to live with them until he came up with a plan.

They heard from traders that Hemlock Bows's woman planned to marry another man. The son decided to visit his mother, and he went to the wigwam where she was living. Hemlock Bows sat nearby looking very sick and sad. His son walked up and asked, "Have you talked her back into staying with you?" Hemlock Bows shook his head. His face was weak, his spirit almost gone, and his legs would not stand.

The son heard a soft crying. He went around the back of the wigwam and found his sister. She was hanging by her hair from a crane on a chimney. She was crying. He climbed up the sloping roof and dropped her down. "Where is dog?" he asked her. She pointed to a tree. There was the dog chewing on an old bone. They all gathered together.

"Father, this woman who is our mother is very evil," said the boy. "She brings pain to those around her and this is not good. It is time for one of us to do something!"

Hemlock Bows hung his head. "I am lost. I do not know what to do. I have provided for that woman. I gave her two children. I brought home fresh meat. She has shunned the ways of our people. I do not know what to do or where to go."

The son pulled two pieces of flint from his pouch. He struck them together, sparked a fire on a dried branch, and threw it into his mother's new wigwam. The wigwam burned to the ground, and the woman with it. The mother's body was found in the ashes. Her head cracked open and an owl flew out screeching.

Hemlock Bows went with his son and daughter to meet the kindly fisherwoman and her daughter. They brought the dog with them, too. Hemlock Bows married the fisherwoman and the family grew well and remained loyal.

11. Monkey-Wife

A Guiana man and his woman once caught a girl monkey and minded her. She became quite tame. When the old people would go away for a while, they would leave the monkey in charge. One day, they went to visit some friends. The monkey took off her skin. She threw it over one of the house-beams and replaced it with an apron. She then cooked a cassava, ate it, and put on her skin again.

When the old couple returned, they searched for the cassava but could not find it. This bothered them, for it was to be their next big meal. They decided to leave someone in their house when they went out again. The old couple went away, leaving a young man hidden behind to watch for anyone who would steal the cassava a second time. After a while, the monkey took off her skin. She put on the apron and started baking the cassava.

The young man rushed up and seized the monkey-woman. He struggled with her. "No," said the monkey-woman, "I am not fit to be your woman."

"But I want you badly!" said the young man.

"That's all very well, but once we are together you will hit me and treat me badly!" The monkey-woman pushed the young man away, but he knelt down on the floor, swearing that he would never hit her. He pleaded with his eyes that he loved her, needed her, and respected her. She felt his compassion and consented to be his woman.

He took her in his arms. He pulled her to him. He treated her with great respect. As she slept, he took the monkey skin down from the beam and burned it in the fire. She awoke and smelled the burning skin. Then she sat and cried in fear that she had made the wrong decision. The young man assured her that his love would never allow him to hurt her.

They lived well for a time. Then the monkey-woman bore the man a boy. The child was small and did not grow as quickly as the other boys in the village. This brought about great pain for the father. He worried about his son. He worried about his monkey-woman. He felt that his son was small because of his monkey-woman, and it made him angry inside.

Things started going badly for them. The man was tired and wished that his son would grow taller and stronger to help with the chores. He had to work hard and then come home and do more work. He started coming home angry, and his anger grew inside of him. He watched his small son play with his monkey-wife. This made him angrier. His anger overtook him and he hit his monkey-wife. She cried out in fear of him. He felt the power of his anger and began to lash her.

The monkey-wife fell upon the floor. Her face filled with terror, and she cried out for him to remember his promise. He let his anger control him. He called her "monkey" and she suffered greatly. Finally, she decided that she could not bear this any longer. She sat in the corner during the night and felt the wisdom to return to her people.

One morning she washed her wounds. She brushed her hair. She took some calabash and some *ite'* starch and told her man that she was going to bathe in the pond. Her man did not work on this day. He watched her out of the corner of his eye. He was relaxed. He did not have to move. He would watch her. She smiled and gathered up her son to wash with her.

She set out toward the pond; instead, she really went far away into the bush. Her man waited for her. He waited and waited and waited, and finally started to search for her. By this time, she was limping along with the help of a stick. Her arms hung by her side, and she was trying her original style of walking on four legs. She was trying to remember how to jump from tree to tree, and her little boy also was leaping. When the husband reached the spot where she had been, he saw her with the boy jumping from tree top to tree top.

"Come back home!" He shouted at her. The monkey-woman took no thought of this. The son felt sorry for his father and threw him spiders and insects to eat. The father could not eat these, and he called to his son, "Come to me! Come home to me!" The son knew of his father's dislike for him, but he threw down more food out of kindness. The father did not understand, and he continued to cry out angrily.

"Come back home!" he called, again and again. The man tried to follow his monkey-wife through the bushes, but she said, "No! I have had enough punishment from you already!"

They went on doing this—the father on the ground running below and the mother and her child jumping from tree to tree. At last they came to a wide river where the monkey cried to her people, the Katannitor, "Come fetch us. We are here!"

They made the wind blow so strongly that it carried the shore closer to the tree where the monkey-woman and her child were. They jumped across, and on reaching the opposite shore became monkeys.

The monkey-woman called to the man, "You must swim after us if you want us!" The little boy called to his father, "Good-bye, I am going!" The mother monkey said nothing more. The man was left on the shore. He went home sadly and destroyed everything that had belonged to the monkey-woman. He cut her hammock, broke her calabash, and smashed her goblets. What a bad temper this man must have had.

12. Miqka'no, Turtle Chief

There was a large camp which was the home of Miqka'no, Turtle Chief. He had a wigwam and land but no one to work for him. So Miqka'no decided that he would look among the women and select one to do his work for him. He found a Menomini woman who was strong, beautiful, plump, and of good spirit. He asked her to be his woman. She stared at him and said, "How are you to provide for a family? You are too slow. You cannot keep with the people!"

Miqka'no smiled. "I can keep with the people. I can move as fast as the young men."

The Menomini woman shook her head. "I think that you should marry an Ottawa woman. They are nearby and they move slowly, as you do."

Miqka'no did not listen. He could not go near the Ottawa people. They were the ones who had turned his people into turtles years before. His group had once been warriors who moved slowly, talked quietly, and were cautious of the un-known. The Ottawa war chief had been tired of urging them on, trying to get them to move, helping them understand. So they were turned into turtles, and Miqka'no was made the head of this turtle group of warriors.

Miqka'no decided to go ahead and make plans for a union party. The Menomini woman delayed the union for as long as possible. Then she decided that to save her honor, she would marry Miqka'no in the spring. Miqka'no at first was delighted, then worried, and then he decided that he needed some time alone. "I must travel with a war party and take some captives," he told her. "This will keep me away until spring. At that time, I expect you to be at the union party." Miqka'no made preparations for the war party. He called together all of his friends, the turtles. He left the camp with his weapons and his turtles. The Menomini woman watched them move and laughed at their slowness.

Miqka'no saw her laughing. "In four days from now you will mourn my distance."

The Menomini woman laughed. "In four days you will scarcely be out of my sight!"

Miqka'no stopped and turned to her. "I did not mean in four days, but four years. Then I shall return!"

The turtles continued to travel until they came to the trunk of a large tree lying in their path. Miqka'no said to his friends, "We cannot go under this trunk. It is too difficult to go over this trunk. It will take too long to go around this trunk. What shall we do?"

One of the turtles said, "Let us burn a hole through the trunk and we can pass through it." This did not work. They thought that perhaps they should return home. It took them a long time.

Once the village was in sight, they began to sing a war song. The villagers ran out to greet them and see their prisoners. The turtles quickly grabbed the people by the wrists and took them as their prisoners.

Miqka'no grabbed the wrist of the Menomini woman. He held her firmly, stating, "You are my prisoner, and now that I have you, I shall keep you as my woman!"

It was traditional to have a ceremony dance to celebrate their victory. When the time arrived, all the turtles put on their costumes. Miqka'no sang and his turtles danced round and round. Miqka'no sang out, "Whoever comes here to see me will die, they will die, they will die, they will die."

At this song the other turtles became afraid. They ran from Miqka'no. They took off their ceremonial clothes and returned to the village. Miqka'no continued to sing. When he realized that everyone had left him, he decided to go to the village. This took him some time, for he did not move very quickly.

Miqka'no entered the village to meet his friends. They approached him with news. "The Menomini woman who was to become yours is married to another man!"

Miqka'no shook his head. He had had a rough time of it. He told his friends, "Let me meet this man." They took him to the Menomini woman's wigwam, and in it he found items that belonged to a man. Miqka'no went outside and waited for the Menomini woman to return. She came to her wigwam with a man, and Miqka'no confronted her. "You promised to be my woman," he said. "You have broken that promise!"

The Menomini woman stared at Miqka'no. "You promised to bring back prisoners. You promised to be gone for four years! What about your promise?"

Miqka'no stared back at the woman. "I did go, and I returned with a number of them." Miqka'no pulled his knife from its sheath and said to the man, "I shall take half of her and you shall take the other half. Both of us shall have part of her, and that should be enough!"

The man was frightened, for he did not want his woman hurt. He gave the woman to Miqka'no, who dragged her away, followed by two long lines of people. He took her to his wigwam. The Menomini woman asked if she could sit quietly and say a prayer, but Miqka'no did not trust her. He watched her as she walked out of the wigwam to a friend's home. She asked to borrow a large kettle, filled it with water, and started to boil this water over the fire. Miqka'no asked. "What are you doing?"

She answered him quietly, "I am warming some water. Do you know how to swim?"

Miqka'no nodded. He liked to swim. The woman then asked him, "This water is to wash you. Your shell is covered with mud. Would you like me to scrub your back and clean your shell?" Miqka'no thought that would be nice. He had had a very difficult day and the mud on his back did itch. The woman lifted Miqka'no. She smiled at him. Miqka'no thought of the beauty of this woman who was now his.

The Menomini woman dumped Miqka'no into the boiling water. He died instantly and sank to the bottom. The other turtles saw this, and saw other people going into their wigwams and getting kettles. They tried to leave but also were killed—and that was the last of them. The Menomini woman returned to her man.

13. Magic Beasts

The Comanches tell of the old days when people walked wherever they went, using dogs to pull the sleds. They had no other way to travel. One day as the people walked, they came upon strange animals that were almost as large as buffaloes. They had long necks, broom tails, and small humps on the backs. There was one large hump reflecting the light of the sun. The people stopped and stared at these strange animals.

One of the animals came up to the Comanche leader, then spoke without opening its mouth. "Who are you?" it asked. "Where are you from?"

As it spoke, the animal split in two. The large, shiny hump that reflected light came off the rest of the body and took on the shape of a man. The other part of the animal then appeared to be the shape of a tall dog. The large, shiny hump part walked to the Comanches like a man, then lifted a part of the shiny lid to reveal a face with an open mouth. Miraculously, a long, shiny, arm-looking part removed some tough skin as fingers lifted to the mouth, pointing to the hollow that held teeth.

The Comanches watched in amazement. Then the shiny hump-man patted his shiny, smooth, tough front that could be considered a stomach area or abdomen. The Comanches watched. The shiny hump-man then made crunching noises with his empty mouth. A Comanche woman who was busy with the children laughed at the shiny hump-man and said, "He wants food. He's hungry." As she walked by, the other part of this strange beast lowered its head to the field grass and began to eat.

The men realized that there was one part of this animal that could feed itself and the other part that needed to be fed. They sent the children off to bring more grass. The men took the grass and stuck it in the shiny hump-man's mouth. It was obvious that this shiny, skinned part could not crawl around on the ground and eat as his other half did. The children placed tall piles of grass in front of the animal of two parts. The shiny hump-man animal spit out the grass. He shook his head. He pointed to his mouth and rubbed his abdomen.

The chief said, "This part may eat meat. Go get him some meat and old bones. He may eat what our dogs eat." The children brought back the throwaway meat they gave the dogs and the old dried bones. The shiny hump-man took the meat in his hand. He made funny sounds and carried the throwaway meat over to the cooking fires, placing it on a green stick. The people watched as this shiny hump-man roasted the meat and then ate it.

More strange, shiny hump-man animals with part-large dog bodies arrived. They separated into two. The large, doglike animals ate the grass and did not speak. The shiny hump-men ate cooked meat. The people did not know what to do with these strange animals. The large dog animals were peaceful enough and could carry much weight. The shiny hump-men were rude, aggressive, and took what meat they wanted. For the throwaway meat did not please them after they saw the good meat. The chief let the hump-men stay with them.

They watched how the shiny hump-men got on and off the magic doglike animals. The shiny hump-people took whatever they wanted from the Comanches. The chief told his people to be quiet and watch.

At last, the shiny hump-people grew tired of staying with the Comanches. They put wrapped ropes around the magic doglike animals and led them around. They tied bundles of the Comaches' food on the rumps of these big dogs. Then they placed hard leather boats on the large dogs and stood up on shiny loops as they mounted the beasts. Now they were one animal again.

The chief called his warriors to him. They followed the strange animals until night. There they saw how the shiny hump-men tied the legs of the large dogs together with the wrapped ropes and guarded them.

The Comanches followed the shiny hump-men until they came to a large adobe village. That night the hump-men tied the legs of the big dogs and let them loose out on the plains. The Comanches braided grass as they waited for the people to sleep.

That night the Comanches crept up on the large dogs. They slipped the grass ropes over the large dogs and led them back to their camp. The large dogs were not fearful of the Comanches, for they had been cared for by them in the past.

The Comanches learned how to ride these large dogs, and they became one of the strongest raiding tribes in the West.

As for the shiny hump-men, they learned to walk.

Afterword

Native American life rose out of the earth and was nurtured within the womb of mythology. Plants, animals, stars, winds, water, fire, and all natural phenomena are integral parts of the human realm. Mysterious spirit powers dwell within all that is. As Ernst Cassirer wrote in *An Essay on Man: An Introduction to a Philosophy of Human Culture,* "The mythical world is at a much more fluid and fluctuating stage than our theoretical world.... The world of myth is a dramatical world, a world of actions, of forces...."

Each story holds the concept of self-contained units that are remnants of episodes in a tribe's history or tradition. Legends, myths, and folktales vary from people to people, depending on the climate, the geography, the food they eat, and the ways they view life and the world around them. All stories in the New World have had the opportunity to overlap and become assimilated into different cultures. The myths are absorbed, collected, and molded into the experiences of those who have taken them on. Many of the myths accepted by one group from another help to illustrate its own versions of creation, survival, and devastation.

Myths can be viewed as magical lenses that help show how the culture was organized, how religious ceremonies came to be, how babies were born, and how honor was bestowed. Myths are not told solely for enjoyment. They are believed.

The thirty-seven myths in this book hold the reflection of the common belief that all were created equal; that all are a living part of the natural earth; that people, men and women, boys and girls, all are equal with the grasses, the winds, the snakes, bears, wolves, and all forms of life. It is believed that all forms of life that exist are bound to one another with a common spirit. This common spirit demands respect, gets respect, or gives punishment.

The common spirit is thought of as a large sphere, or circle. The circle is never-ending. It is illustrated among the Pueblos as two snakes swallowing each other's tails, and it goes on and on and on and on. Human beings are part of this circle, or chain, that holds all the forms of life. The bear, the wolf, the deer, the birds, the tiniest insect, the flower—they are all related and equal. No one is better or stronger; we are all equal in power and spirit strength.

The cycle of life begins with the birth of a child. Many times the birth comes about from a spiritual conception. The child is then put through severe testings or adopted by a wise one. The wise one can be an animal, a chief, or a spirit that has the ability to teach great knowledge to this spiritually conceived child. The myths follow his adventures in the learning of light, rivers, and animals. There is a constant concern for the beginning of life and the foundation of the world in which all beings live.

The native American hero or adventurer can change into any shape that he wants or make himself into anything he wants. His spirit power comes to him from the Earth and the Sky. The testings place the hero against other spirits. Native American people believe that one can speak to animals and they will respond. Horrible ghosts, monsters, and enemies can take any shape to test spirit strength.

The testings of spirit strength also relate to the testing of love. Human lovers can take on different shapes and can go through unbelievable feats to prove their truths. Alliances between lovers and animals occur. The beauty of the love testing is that love and sex are considered sacred among The People. If a woman performs a sexual act unknowingly with a snake, for example, she is bound to that snake forever. That union brings them together; they belong together. A romantic version of this is the European story of *Beauty and the Beast.* The exchange of love brings a sacred trust and tolerance.

As with the emotion of love, laughter, sadness, and curiosity are all important philosophies of The People. There is a belief that native Americans who have been dealt a poor hand need laughter to survive.

This book illustrates the wonder of transformation. Animals are part of life; therefore, animals are part of the myths. The medicine, emblems, creators, and tricksters are animals as well as humans. There is no division between animals and people. An elder at one pueblo talks to the birds; and when an anthropologist asked him about this, he laughed and said, "In your Bible you have a wise woman who talked with a snake. I talk with the hawks, eagles, and swallows."

All cultures across the Americas tell of bears, wolves, deer, snakes, and other animals with their wisdom. Some human beings become animals in order to provide food for their hungry people. Some humans become animals because the people are bad and the only way to continue good is to change shape. Animals and people through myths have found a bond to live together in mutual harmony and respect.

Exchanges between the living and the dead happen through myths. Sometimes men and women find that their loves are ghosts. Testings are given, true love found, and most often the dead one must return to the place of the dead. The rituals continue, and the story behind the ritual keeps the ceremonies alive. The myths live on as sung in a traditional Tewa chant for the dead:

WE have sent the smoke for you
WE have cast the charcoal on the ground between us
WE have made deep world lines between us
Do not come back for us
Send us spirit strength to gain wisdom
Long life that our children will grow
Give us food and crops
And in all the spirit of The People
WE ask for this and nothing more
Now go, go, for you are free.

Story Notes

The beauty of the words lies in the telling of the tales—a telling that gives life to each story's truth. Here are the tellers of the truths.

Thunder Son   Dark lines creased a weathered and tanned face. The left eye closed with the breath of each sentence. Elwyn TallHands guided his hands through the air, shaping the body of a man with long, black hair. The sleek, muscular body of the man in the story is reflected in Elwyn's eyes. Perhaps Elwyn once was this man, the snake-man who could turn from snake to man and back again.

The beating of the drums at the Social Dance could be heard off in the distance at the Santo Domingo Pueblo. The bandana around his head gave Elwyn an air of elegance. He was elegant, for he was the grandfather of many and the holder of stories. His father was Algonquin, belonging to the linguistic group of families of North American Indians. Elwyn spoke of his father as being a mix of Blackfoot and Ojibway, the latter being one of the most prolific of symbol writers upon the rock, sand, hide, and sky. Elwyn was a holder, a powerful holder, who was taught to remember the stories of the old ones and the old ways.

Elwyn TallHands had been brought to the Santo Domingo Pueblo Social Dance by a friend who felt Elwyn would enjoy seeing others' ways. Elwyn became sad for his own people. He would not speak of his move to Oklahoma and then to Albuquerque, New Mexico. He would not talk about his family or his friend.

The friend who had brought him was a new friend whom he had met only a short time ago in the city and could drive. Elwyn and I met at the snowcone table. He was buying a cherry snowcone and did not have enough money to pay. I was buying four snowcones for my kids, and was willing to pay for Elwyn's since he was polite enough to help me carry all the snowcones back to the children.

"You know of these people?" he had asked me while the ice melted in the hot July sun. "Yes. These people are of my people." I spoke softly, for now we were walking down by the ditch away from people, away from the magic of the dances, into the peace and quiet of the easy-moving ditch water.

"Do you know stories of the people?" He knew now that I knew what he needed to share, a story.

Elwyn TallHands' ageless face reflected his story as he told it in the shade of an old adobe home. The ditch gurgled as the horses walked through it, slurping at the fresh, cool water. People were milling around by the hundreds. Where we sat there was just Elwyn, me, and the story of Thunder Son.

Spirit Eggs   The Cheyenne are known as one of the warring tribes of the Algonquin who once roamed between the Missouri and Arkansas rivers. David Alcoze, who was a Cheyenne Indian and proud of his heritage, had asked me to Dallas to share native American stories with his group. He was eager to build up the Indian Art Museum near the Dallas Natural History Museum. David's wife Cynthia works with the Indian Council trying to hold The People together in harmony and pride.

The plane that I was to fly home on to Albuquerque was late by an hour. The airport outside of Dallas was busy with people. There were children milling around looking for food or fights with each other. Parents sat with stone faces staring into space. Couples wrapped around each other in supportive embraces. I was alone, thinking about the people there, when a large Indian woman sat down beside me and introduced herself as Sonia Broom.

Sonia Broom nudged my right arm. "Would you like one?" She pointed a roll of wintergreen lifesavers at me. "Thank you." I took the roll and carefully removed one round bicycle-tire candy. She took the roll back and nudged me again with her elbow. "All these people are going somewhere. Where are you going?" I told her, watching the smile grow on her face.

"I am not going home," she said. "I am going to a meeting in Oklahoma where the people get together and share. There are mountain men there who think that they are mountain men. Some are, some aren't, but they have a good time. That's what is important." She popped another wintergreen candy into her mouth.

Chewing, she asked where I was born and I told her. Sonia Broom told me that she was Cheyenne. The people were losing their culture, their strength, their knowledge of themselves. "Language holds the way of the people, and when the people forget their language—they forget who they are." Sonia spoke in her own tongue for a while to prove her point.

"People change when they listen to the Spirits, and people change when they don't." Sonia worked her way through the full roll of wintergreen lifesavers as she told this story of the Spirit Eggs. When she had finished the story, she had eight children sitting at her feet and four adults, all of whom were captivated.

"Sonia Broom, thank you for your story."

Snake-Boy   Leslie Codu told this story at a powwow in Albuquerque. Leslie sold medicine pipes for his uncle. Leslie would not say if he was Cherokee or not, but his uncle was. This is Leslie's story. I have not heard from him since, nor do I know where he is now. Thank you for the story, Leslie. May you be well.

Water Monster Snake-Man   Alex and Patti Apostolides tell stories on KTEP Radio out of El Paso and do field research while not writing, selling real estate, or educating the world. They invited us to go to Alamo Canyon and review an Apache ceremonial site. Alex was magically in love with one particular panel and he begged me to try to find out the story behind the symbols.

This sparked an interest in the Apache myths. Alex and Patti made a life-size copy of the petroglyph symbol site. They were very careful not to touch or harm the actual abraded symbols in any way. This long, long, thirty-foot roll of plastic with drawings was then given to me. I took it to various meetings and gatherings in hopes of hearing the story behind the drawings. It was not noticed or accepted at most of these public events. At a school, I mentioned to the kids that I had this long roll of plastic with drawings on it and no one knew what they meant. Their assignment would be to write on the meanings of these symbols.

The next day I brought Alex and Patti's long plastic symbol drawing. I put it up in the classroom and let the students get a feel of its beauty. Two days later the written assignments came pouring in, laid neatly on my desk. Stapled to one of the papers was a short note that invited me to visit a student's home. The invitation brought conversation, and pain from past suffering became apparent as the story unfolded. The story was told with the illustration of each symbol made obvious. The words did not fit the symbols, but the feelings did. One must know the feelings of the people to know the strength of their symbols.

This particular story is not on a petroglyph panel that I know. The story was shared while many of the Apache stories were explained. The downfall of the people was not due solely to the inhumane treatment of the U.S. military. Some of it came from the aggression of the Plains Indians.

I cannot divulge the name of the student or the teller, but the story became known. The story has now been confirmed by many people who remembered it once they heard. Thank you, Alex and Patti, for bringing the story back to life. Thank you for helping the people remember.

Rattlesnake Father   The Pomo people hold magic in their eyes. Susan Povi Baugh and I drove non-stop to Tempe, Arizona, to attend a National Pictographic Conference. The conference was a sharing of understanding related to the awareness of symbol writing on rocks, caves, hides, sandpaintings, etc. Boma Johnson of the Yuma, Arizona, office of the Bureau of Land Management was there and gave his talk on tremendous arrangements of rocks that lay out on the desert floor in the shape of human beings and other forms. Boma Johnson explained that many anthropologists had no idea what these rocks were doing way out there until someone took a photo of them from the air. Then their shapes became apparent. They were huge symbols put there for a purpose.

Susan and I had very little time to visit after the conference, for we had to drive home to families that were waiting. The Tonto Apache National Forest was on our map. We drove through the thick forest of trees, which last year was seriously damaged by fire. There was a little store in town that sold hot drinks and fresh pie. We pulled over. On our walk up the road, we came to a store that had everything in it. There were Indian paintings, Mexican pottery, earrings from India, earrings from the Sioux, French perfume, mugs from Hong Kong, and cards from Chicago that were printed in Italy.

The woman who stood behind the counter asked about our trip. We told her about Boma Johnson's rock symbols. She showed Susan and me a six-foot shield that her father had made. It was woven in a delicate weave. When I asked if there was a story behind the snake symbols, her voice lifted. "Yes, if you have time for a story…"

Woman Seeker   The story of White Corn is a well-known myth that is taught and told throughout the Southwest. The power of the story is held in the way of the telling. Each teller has his or her own techniques for relating the information. My telling of this story comes from a Grandfather at Oraibi in the Navam-sma family. Grandfather told this story to my two little girls when they were seven and nine. The images they remember, but the story they have forgotten over time.

Here, then, is the story of White Corn for you to share and know. Your version shall be your own to hold, change, or treasure. Each part of the story is of utmost importance and holds parts of some ceremonies in it.

Water Jar Boy The story of the Water Jar Boy is well known. In the Plains it is know as the story of Buffalo Dung Boy. The power of the story has been studied and written about even by Joseph Campbell. The morality of The People is reflected in this tale. The Indian Pueblo Cultural Council in Albuquerque recorded on video-tape my telling of this tale to the elders, who nodded at each turning point. This lets the storyholder know that he or she is telling it in agreement with what everyone knows. Each person tells the story differently; however, the major points must be remembered in proper sequence, for changing their order changes the meaning of the story.

The hero who is born of the water jar ends up in search of his true father. This one was in search of, seeking towards, wanting knowledge of, his true father. This story brings the son to his true father, and in the end the search for this man unites the family again in the right and proper place.

Sacred Snake Geronima Montoya taught me when I was little that what you see may not be real. This story reflects the power of what one needs and what may come from those needs. The beauty of the young woman brought about a hungry need for the sacred spring water. The sacred spring held her path from there.

"You are born good, you are born perfect, you are born as you should be." Geronima Montoya taught that if you do what you believe is good, right, and whole, then your life shall be good, right, and whole. This woman in the story brought about her way through her own decision to do something unique on her own. Geronima Montoya holds the sparkle of this story in her eyes.

Greedy Brothers The family unit is one of the strongest forces on this planet. The strength comes not from the blood line, not from the parents, but from the ability for each person to work for the good of the whole family. To be able to work together with siblings is a strong factor among The People. Each is equal and the same. And each is noticeably different, able to perform different tasks, have different abilities, and have different ways of looking at life.

The sum total of all the family brings about a unity of caring, working together, and sharing. If that unity is broken, bad will come to that family, perhaps even death. Families are sacred—each family that lives next door is sacred—and if there is a problem, they all come together and support The Group.

This story is from Asqwueth David Davis, who is Sioux. He had seven brothers and eight sisters and lived north of Taos until he moved back to Oklahoma. He teaches through his stories and says that if you listen to them, you need to continue to tell, for no story should go untouched.

Ghost Hunter   Helene Healing-Woman said that her mother was Dakota. Her father was Navaho. She worked at a store in Shiprock and told us this story one night late after a healing ceremony we had been to near Lukachukai, Arizona. Helene Healing-Woman only worked on people she knew for at least four or five years. She was the holder of the sacred knife that brought about clear visions of people's path.

She held great wisdom and healing. She worked on the healing way from Acoma to Utah and was widely known as the *Yaya-titcra* of the bad illness, or heart trouble with diabetes. She died three years ago when the pickup she was driving was hit head-on north of Thoreau, New Mexico. Her granddaughter tells some stories, but is very shy and prefers to speak in Navaho.

White Wolf Woman   White Wolf Woman is a story that goes back to the beginning of time. The White Wolf Woman is still seen to this day. An anthropology professor came from the East Coast and rode down White Wolf Canyon with his twenty-one-year-old son and the son's girlfriend. The snow came down unexpectedly and they were trapped in the blinding cold snowstorm. As they rode toward the west search-ing frantically for a way out, there appeared on the horizon of the canyon wall a howling white wolf. He said that when he blinked, the image changed to a woman with long, flowing hair that was tied with white feathers. She was pointing to the north gorge.

He turned to see the direction in which she was pointing, and when he looked back to thank her, she was gone. He tried to find her and rode up the cliff path while his son and son's girlfriend rode out for help. The professor had a camera, and when he reached the top flat plain and looked out, all he saw was a long, thin white wolf loping away from him. The white wolf had white feathers tied in its mane.

The professor took photos of the paw prints and had them analyzed. The lab could not identify the type of Lupus that had left the prints.

Wolf-Chief's Son   Tlingit Indians mingled around the New Mexico State Fair in 1987. They were dressed the same as everyone else and were basically not noticed—until they started to talk. There were seven of them, all men, all very interested in the native American myths I was telling at the State Fair. They told me their names, which I could not pronounce and cannot remember. They told the story together. One man would tell the story until he was tired or finished with his part, and then he would nod to another fellow who would then continue on until he was tired. It was a circle story, and the ending was finished by the first teller. Here, then, is their story.

Three Mountain Wolf-Water Monster   The Chiricahua Apache were a misunderstood group of people who roamed the plains. At times they were with the Kiowa or the Comanche, but they always looked out after their own. The women held great powers among the Apache. Lozen, the great Apache Warrior Woman, held special talents both as a warrior and as a healer. The U.S. Government at one time offered a generous reward to anyone who would bring in "dead or alive" an Apache warrior or woman.

This story is found on the rocks near Three Sisters Mountain in southern New Mexico. The spirit world is still strong here in the Southwest, with the awareness that there are many dimensions one can function in and see. The "knowing how" and the "acceptance of" are the most important abilities.

Wolf Star   "People came from the whirlwind bag," a Pawnee Indian, Robert Shosho, said. "The Pawnee people took a very long time to understand good ways from bad ways. Their heads were in a whirl when they were created and it took a thousand years for them to walk straight. Many do not like the Pawnee to this day, because we eat of the Raw Liver. Some say that we eat of the Raw Liver to help us remember life back in the whirlwind bag."

The whirlwind bag of Paruksti held the creation of birth, the existence of life, and the naming of the people. Paruksti was a spirit that could transform life from nothing into something. He even made the

Wolf People. The ability of the Wolf People is magical, and they work with the stars and the night visions.

Wolf Woman Running   Carolota Shange told this story at a woman's healing smoke. Carolota was Sioux and she remembers being taken from the reservation by missionaries who shaved her head, poured kerosene on her naked scalp, and left her crying on a church pew by the school with forty other kids. She believes in Christianity enough to say that the best Christians she ever met have never stepped in a church or tried to change someone else's way.

The first time I heard this story from her, I thought it was about her. It isn't. It is a common story about bravery, and I believe there was such a woman who existed, for this story is recorded with the Federal Government. Carolota Shange is now one hundred and four years old and still tells stories. She does not go outside for fear that she will be taken against her will from her home, as she was when she was a child on the reservation.

She lives south of Albuquerque on a chicken farm with her grandson and eight grandchildren. She helps me with my stories and asks all young people to call her "Grandmother."

Medicine Wolf   Blackfeet do not call themselves Blackfeet. Some call them "the Blackfoot," but the Blackfeet call themselves the "Satsika Indians." They are Plains Indians once known for their stealing and trading of women. This particular woman learned ways of trusting those she did not know and was transformed from being dependent on others into being her own person. At the end, this story deals with the concept that death is not the end of life but its continuation on a different level.

Ramos Burnside tells this story, leaving the ending as an unknown. When Sits-By-The-Door becomes very ill at the end of the tale, Ramos ends the story. The listener is left to decide Sits-By-The-Door's outcome. It is believed that one cannot go through a tremendous testing in life and not have some death of the old ways and birth of the new ways. Inside each of us, every day, there is change, transformation, rebirth of hope.

Wolf Daughter   White Sheet-To-Wind tells this story at her gatherings in Utah. She is an old grandmother who has more children than all the Spirits combined. Her duty to each of us, as her grandchildren, is to tell the stories that hold the processes of life.

The Eskimo daughter in this story is flexible. She not only changes into a wolf, but marries an otter and gives birth to unique individual animals that are able to be accepted on their own. This Eskimo daughter is manipulative. She gets food for everyone, tricking her otter husband into doing for her by using her pouting, her love, and her support. This is truly a woman of all emotions who can carry it off and win favor with all. The concept of changing into an animal that has all of these traits is wonderful, even if the story is something that we cannot achieve!

White Sheet-To-Wind comes down in the winter, for that is the storytelling time. Otherwise she is up north by Juneau, Alaska, resting, telling, and being a grandmother to all who come her way.

The Boy and the Bear   Bear clans are strong throughout the continent. They are run solely by women in some areas, and in others no one but elderly men can enter. Each tribe has its own rules, its own secrets, and its own bear clan. Rosa deVida was on the Iroquois Cattaraugus Reservation and she knew the chants of the old ones. She knew of the ways of the old ones and she knew the ways of the Baptist Church.

The Baptist Church brought her freedom from her overbearing mother-in-law and gave Rosa deVida an opportunity to sing songs like the meadowlark at dawn. Rosa deVida loved hymns, loved people, and loved to express herself. She was very upset that the Bible did not say if bears were allowed in heaven, for she was herself part bear.

Rosa deVida sang songs at a local church with a group that was traveling around from Ohio. She then proceeded to tell stories of her people at the coffee afterward. The students I had taken to hear the songs (for a class critique) were amazed to know that Rosa deVida still believed in the ways of her people, also believed in the way of the Baptists. Life is filled with patterns, colors, and beliefs that can be shared. Listen and you will feel Rosa deVida's world come to life...

Bear-Mother   Vanity is warned against in all cultures. Being vain holds a certain amount of danger. Regardless of the self-love, there is danger that causes one to lose perspective of who one really is. Grandmother Running Rabbit's advice is that arrogance is the greatest downfall of all mankind. She never had that trouble, but she must know, for she speaks with strict words.

The Haida teller of this story was a friend of Grandmother Running Rabbit. Her story was reflected in her eyes, and watching them as she described the Bear-Chief's wife, you could see what she saw.

Beast Bear-Man   Richard and Judy Young came to visit on New Year's Day, 1989, and did a storytelling in the library at Santa Fe. I sat in the audience ready to hear wonderful Arkansas stories roll out through the New Mexico air. Once the telling was over, people gathered round them to get tapes and books.

One older man moved to sit next to me. He asked if I knew Richard and Judy and I told him that I did. He proceeded to tell me about his life and his travels. As the people talked and shared with the Youngs, this older man told me his story of the Beast Bear-Man. When he finished, he stood up and left.

Bearskin-Woman   "Respect your elders or they will turn on you. Respect those who know more than what you think they know, for they have wisdom that can overcome emotion. If you give respect, you shall receive respect." The gravel voice barked out in the night air. The sheep were in the makeshift corral near the sandstone escarpment. We had started out with only eight people herding sheep. When we stopped at dusk, to build a fire and read from a book, fourteen more faces arrived.

Hot coffee heated in a tin coffee pot was always kept full. There was always a cup ready and a story to be shared. In the morning, there would be only the eight of us again.

"Respect, knowing that if you do not know what to do, ask someone that you respect." Gnarled old fingers shook at the red-orange flames of the fire. Stars sparkled overhead. Crisp, cold night air echoed the sound of the old one's voice. His wisdom was here, his wisdom was going to be shared, and he would be respected.

Bear-Man   Pawnee people moved around once, trying to find a place that was their own. They were displaced and traveled by horse to wherever they could find food. They were not accepted by very many, for they were born of whirlwind and were confused about respect and rude behavior. The Pawnee may not have had their own land, but they did have their own stories. This Pawnee story was told by a Zuni man who had known the Pawnee teller of this tale.

The Zuni man did not want his name mentioned, for he did not want anyone to know that he had shared time with a Pawnee. But then he said, "Every group has good and bad. Every group has different people in it, except the Pawnee." Here is a good story, and I am glad that the Zuni man remembered it to share with you.

Ma'nabush and the Bear   The Rain priest brought his cane to the ceremony. He had held it in his hand all morning, and as the sun moved across the sky, the cane appeared to have grown. Several people had remarked on this.

The Rain priest only spoke to those of his same sex and age. "What appears to be seen is not what is." The Rain priest told this story, and when he was finished he took his cane, put it in the green Ford truck, and drove away. This, then, is his story. I do not know about the cane.

Porcupine vs. Thunderers   The Iroquois are members of the Five Nations. Tribes within the Iroquois that speak Algonquian are the Huron, Wyandot, Seneca, Mohawk, Tuscarora, Oneida, Cayuga, Ononadaga, and Cherokee.

An Iroquois teller, White Running Turtle, told this story to my oldest daughter and me when we were on a research trip to Chaco Canyon. White Running Turtle was visiting there with his two sons who were only three and five years of age. He thought the trip would be good so his wife could have time alone and he could be with his sons. He hadn't planned on their being so active, not sleeping, and being constantly hungry. We teamed up with him to give him some time out. My daughter Nicole looked after the boys while he and I went for a walk and talked about how different each culture is and how similar we are.

This story came from his family, and he was most proud to teach me both the English word and the Algonquin word for porcupine. Thunderers is a guttural word that was very hard for me to pronounce. White Running Turtle told of his people, the Tuscarora, and how diluted they are. He was most proud of remembering at least some of his family's language. His Hi-nua strongly resembles him, and perhaps the old man in the story took on some of the character of his two sons. When the story was over, White Running Turtle showed me how to fly with Thunder wings.

White Hawk   White Hawk Smith is six feet, eight inches tall and weighs all of two hundred and ten pounds. He is solid muscle, wears moccasins, and avoids people who spit tobacco. This is his story. He is the only one I know of who tells it.

This story is a trial of love that surpasses the most complex of relationships. White Hawk Smith claims to be a Shawnee and he probably is. Even though his hair is red and his eyes green, his blood is Shawnee.

Seneca Medicine   Mannie Cedric Gabaldon is a purist who tells stories of the way of medicine. Medicinal herbs are the oldest technique of healing among Indian people. The Old Ones tell of a time when the people came to this place. It was prepared for them. Plants grew in abundance, animals thrived, and the water was clean. The plants were gifts from the Spirits. The wisdom of how to use the plants came from the learning of the people. Some people survived, some people died, and most of us learned well. Mannie Cedric Gabaldon is a healer of the Old Ways and feels with all his spirit that to heal others, you need to *believe* that you can heal. To be cured by others, you need to *believe* that you can be cured. To have a vision is to find your own power. The story holds the power to open your power to heal.

Gopher's Wisdom   Chew-chew Raven talks slowly. At the end of each sentence he pauses for the listener to say, "Hey-yah." He then moves to the next sentence. Chew-chew Raven tells a story slowly, like the river water feeling its way around each rock. Not only feeling a way around each rock, but feeling each tiny niche in the rock, as if to remember the rock forever. Chew-chew Raven has purple-black hair long to his ankles, and has dark chocolate-brown eyes with soft specks of grey in them. His lips curl slightly down as he tells; his eyes carefully watch his hands that lie on his lap unmoving.

Chew-chew Raven wears his beaded low moccasins with honor and pride. He won them at a powwow in Texas one year. They are not worn at all, which makes one wonder if he walks when he wears them. Yet he must walk, for he wears them all the time, every day, and he has walked with me.

Chew-chew Raven is soft-spoken. He is fragile with his sensitive character, yet strong in muscle strength. He is six feet easy and weighs in at around one hundred and sixty pounds. He chops cedar beams for a living, makes traditional ceilings, and speaks softly. His stories are always of women's troubles—where a woman gets an innocent man into a trial. The women are forgotten no sooner than mentioned, but the man's trial goes on and on, "Hey-yah."

Wolf Clan Lesson   The Nass River people of the Northwest coast survived unbelievable natural traumas. Colie Flatblanket and Carrie Roundfish came to the pueblo for a meeting of women. We were going to have a woman's ceremony and they were down here trying to sell smoked salmon and catch stories. They were obliged in both endeavors.

Colie Flatblanket told this story while Carrie Roundfish nodded, smiled, and shook her finger as the tale spun its way into our world.

Colie Flatblanket has crystal-blue eyes that appear to be opaque. Her hair is black, her skin white as milk, and her voice booming and strong. She stands all of five feet, three and weighs no more than the four packs of fifty-pound salmon. At the telling of the salmon with the burning pitch, she cried. The fire and the lava from the high volcano brought more tears. The ending of the story brought a strong anger. Her story doesn't end, so she said, for the salmon are still trying to gain their freedom and rise to the surface.

Buffalo-Maiden Sitting Pretty Buffalo is one hundred and eleven years old last July. Sitting Pretty Buffalo still wears the traditional garb of her Arikara people. She is blind, speaks carefully, and stops frequently to hear her audience grunt. That way she knows you are still there, still awake, and still listening.

Sitting Pretty Buffalo lives in a trailer court near Rio Rancho, New Mexico. Her granddaughter was in one of my creative writing classes and did very well. Granddaughter won an award for outstanding Native American Story from the *Albuquerque Journal* newspaper.

Sitting Pretty Buffalo tells of her people with a voice that speaks through the vision of hard years. Sitting Pretty Buffalo's man was once a strong and powerful leader. He died when she was thirty-nine years old. She has been loyal and loving to him all this time. As she says in her own words, "I have left him to go on, and my mourning keeps me in happy thoughts of his warm touch." Here is Sitting Pretty Buffalo's story of love.

KoKo Wisdom *KoKo* in the Keres language is the word for coconut. The original name was *Kow'a*, with a harsh, guttural "w"; somehow the name was changed. *Kow'a* means cornhusk, or one who has the knowledge of the corn's health by knowing of the cornhusk. Uncle Julian Lo' tells this story. He tells of how the men take the fertility from their being (represented by corn kernals, which they plant in the ground). The nurturing Sky Father (male Spirit identity) drops his water upon the earth (female Spirit identity), and the kernals sprout and grow. The men are the caretakers of the corn (takes on female child identity). When the corn has grown and the ears are ready to be picked (young, fertile, maiden Spirit identity), the men pick the ears, singing praises to the Spirits.

The night that it is picked the men roast the corn in an underground pit. The head father of the home takes the corn to his woman in the dawn light. It is his gift of life to her. She has borne him children; he has borne her corn food to feed them. She cooks the corn. He takes the first bite of the ear of cooked corn and passes the ear to his right. Each member of the household takes a bite of the corn, careful to leave the last kernals for the head father to finish. When he finishes off the last of the corn kernals on that ear, everyone knows life is as it should be.

Uncle Julian Lo' was a medicine man for many years. He now lives in the suburbs of Salt Lake City, Utah. He taught stories for eighteen years and I hope he is still telling wherever he is.

Faithless Woman   "Talk about having trouble. You talk about having trouble! Trouble?! You don't even begin to know about trouble! Wait until you hear about Hemlock Bows. That's Trouble!" Harry Charles Baldonado, Jr., shook his head. He heard my story of life's ups and downs and he smiled through my sad tale. His response was blunt. His story was long, but then everything Harry Charles Baldonado does takes time—good time, rich time, but lots of time.

Monkey-Wife   The Guiana people rarely get this far north. However, there was a nurse at the co-operative in Tierra Amarilla who had worked for eleven years in Guiana. She missed the people and their humor. We appreciated her hard work out in the rural medical field here in New Mexico, and a group of us had decided to take her to dinner at the local cantina. She rewarded us with this most unusual story.

Listening to this story of the jungle while staring out at the open plains of New Mexico brought about a strange sensation. Marriage, though, regardless of location can also bring about a strange sensation. May your marriage be good and your story as life-rich.

Miqka'no, Turtle Chief   "If you were a turtle chief, would you consider it an honor? If you were a turtle chief and had to prove your honor, would you go to war? If you were a turtle chief and had to prove your manhood to a woman, would you be strong and fearless?" Tortulio Manzanares glared at the young man standing next to me. "Well, what would you do?"

The young man looked down and said nothing. "Nothing? Would you do nothing?" Tortulio lifted the young man's chin with his fingers. "I am talking to you and you are not deaf. What would you do?" The young man studied Tortulio's face. Tortulio was anxious for an answer, but his face gave no hint as to what he expected. We knew Tortulio and Tortulio was a trickster. What one might think to say would only make

Tortulio laugh. The young man smiled. "You tell me what the turtle chief would do."

Tortulio nodded his head and turned to me. "This one is smart. You trained him well. I'll tell you what, I will tell you exactly what the turtle chief did and then you will know. How's that?"

Magic Beasts   Andy Anaya has the best tamales in all of the Southwest. He also has the finest Indian jewelry; and well he should, for Galisteo, New Mexico, started out as an Indian settlement before the Spanish took it over, only to abandon it. Then the miners came and mined the hills of all the turquoise they could find, and when the vein dried up, the hills collapsed with the lack of care. The hippies arrived to find it a peace-filled haven. Hog Farm and Easy Rider cruised through Galisteo. Then the old western bars were opened to movie productions such as *Young Guns.*

Andy Anaya and his family are Spanish, but the loyalty has shifted from Government loyalty to People loyalty. Sit back, have a tamale, and here's the story. . .